# Indecision

Elisabeth Grace

Cover design and photo by: Damonza
Developmental Editor: Angela Smith
Line Editor: Megan Hand
Proof Reader: Behind The Writer

ISBN: 1987925025
ISBN-13: 978-1-987925-02-9

# DEDICATION

To all the first responders who put their lives on the line so we don't have to. Thank you!

# Indecision

# Chapter One

## Jackie

"Damn it." I threw my hands in the air and kicked the flat tire with my sneaker.

My runner's high was quickly evaporating, being stuck on the side of a country road with a flat, no phone, and the sun beating down on my shoulders. I was starting to think that leaving the tourist-filled sidewalks of Bar Harbor to jog on the quiet country roads hadn't been such a great idea. I glanced around at the rolling hills of the countryside. It could be an hour before someone happened upon me on this road. I supposed I was going to have to give changing the damn tire a try.

Sighing, I opened the driver's door and hit the button to pop the trunk, then made my way to the back of the car. I pulled the trunk open and released another aggravated breath. The back of my car was packed full of cases of beer, all containing empty bottles. I'd been meaning to get around to returning them, but regretfully—at that moment anyway—I hadn't gotten there yet.

I was a party girl, but these weren't all *my* empties.

My best friend, Chloe, had broken up with her douchebag of a boyfriend a couple months before, after she'd found him sampling his secretary on the desk in his office, so I'd thrown a get together in a last ditch effort to show her there was plenty of fun still to be had and plenty of available men on the market.

I should know—I worked with a good portion of them, being a 911 Operator. Eligible cops, EMTs, and firefighters were a part of my existence, and I knew one of them would be my friend's remedy to take her mind off her troubles. Unfortunately, Chloe hadn't felt the same.

I pulled the cases of beer and empty wine bottles out of the trunk and placed them on the shoulder of the road, then pulled up the carpet of the trunk to expose the spare tire and other equipment. Setting the jack and tire wrench on the ground, I wrestled the tire out of the trunk. And what a wrestle it was, seeing as it was big, and I was tiny, and it was an all-around awkward thing to hold on to. Letting the tire drop onto the pavement, I wiped the sweat off my forehead with my forearm.

A half hour later, I'd managed somehow to figure out the jack and lift the car up enough that I would probably be able to remove the flat. Score one for me! Now all I had to do was loosen these nuts, take the ruined tire off, slide the new one on, replace the nuts, and I'd be good to go. Easy peasy.

*I am female, hear me motherfucking roar.*

Triumph surged through me as I picked up the tire wrench and placed it over the first nut, attempting to turn it. It didn't budge. Hmm. That sucker was on good. I tried again, putting a little more oomph into it, but it still didn't nudge. Like, not even a little. Had Hercules put these damn things on or what?

Inhaling a deep breath and trying to brush off my mounting frustration, I tried once more, this time leaning all my body weight into it. Still nothing.

Okay, this was okay, I told myself. I'd just come back to that one. I placed the wrench over another of the bolts and tried to loosen it. Again it didn't budge.

*Aargh!*

Fed up, I threw the tire wrench in the dirt, punched my car with the side of my fist, and screamed, my frustration finally bubbling over.

That's when I heard the sound of tires slowly rolling over the dirt coming from behind me. I turned to see a police car parking on the shoulder.

A sigh left my mouth and I hunched my shoulders down in defeat. Great. I was all for getting help, but I didn't even want to think of the ribbing I'd take if the guys from work found out I'd been a helpless female at the side of the road in need of help. Hopefully it was someone I knew well enough to convince them to keep their mouth shut.

I stood from my crouch and watched the door open. He was tall and muscular as evidenced by the way his black police uniform stretched across his chest and at the sleeves. His hair was longish and sandy brown with a slight curl at the ends. Instead of looking messy and unkempt, it suited him perfectly, curling up over his ears and at the base of his neck in a sexy way.

Nope, I definitely didn't know this guy. If I'd ever seen him before he would've been on my radar and had it pinging like crazy—there was no chance I'd forget him. And now I'd meet him for the first time covered in dried sweat. Awesome. Thank God for extra-strength deodorant.

Speaking of that radar, the pinging was becoming more intense as he sauntered over to my car. Ping......ping....ping...ping...ping, ping, ping, ping, ping, ping.

As he drew nearer, I saw that his eyes were gray—no wait, they were green. Now they were gray again. I wasn't sure what damn color his eyes were because they kept changing every time the sun hit them a different way.

He wore a small smirk, his lips tilting up at the corners. "Seems you've run into a bit of trouble," he said, then gave my body a full perusal. He must've liked what he saw because his grin was even wider when he finished. My sports bra and running tights felt entirely too small all of a sudden.

I spared a glance away from his intoxicating eyes and read his name badge.

*J. McTavish*

Wait, I did know this guy. He'd transferred into the department a few months ago. Jamie. I'd never met him, but I'd sent him on some calls, the most recent of which was last week.

"I did," I said in a friendly way. "And I left my cell phone at home."

He nodded and gave a sidelong glance to the pile of empties sitting beside the car. His forehead scrunched, and he moved his hands to rest on top of his utility belt. "Any reason for those?" He nodded toward the pile.

My face heated. Great first impression I was making. "They were in my trunk, and I needed to pull them out to get to my spare." I motioned with my hand to the donut tire lying in the dirt.

"You've haven't by any chance been drinking, have you, ma'am?" His eyebrows drew in.

My eyes narrowed. *Did he seriously just call me ma'am? Do I look like a ma'am to him?* I mean, sure, I had an hour's worth of sweat on me from my run, and I was probably covered in dust and dirt from trying to change this stupid tire, but I was nowhere close to the point in my life that some prick police officer should be referring to me as a ma'am.

"My name is—" I started off haughtily before he

interrupted me.

"Just answer the question ma'am," he said with a stern tone.

There he went again! I heaved out an exaggerated sigh. "No, I haven't been drinking. It's only lunch time for God's sake."

His eyes narrowed. "There's no reason to be difficult. Just answer the question when I ask it."

I bit the inside of my cheek to keep from saying something I'd probably regret, given the fact that I'd have to deal with him on occasion at work.

"What's your name?" he asked in that flat, monotone way that cops did from time-to-time.

"Jackie," I returned in the same tone.

"Jackie what, ma'am? Let's not make this encounter more problematic than it has to be."

*Ugh.* Why had I pushed? I knew from his tone that he was losing patience with me, but I'd always bucked authority. I didn't know why—it was just me.

It wasn't like I'd never had to deal with a police officer before. I mean, I'd been pulled over for speeding and stuff, but they all knew me around here. Not only through work, but because I'd lived in Bar Harbor my whole life. I'd never actually had to play my 'I'm one of you' card before.

I crossed my arms over my chest. "Jackie Davenport."

His eyes dipped to the center of my chest where my cleavage was pushed together. Parting my lips, I inhaled a deep breath. I decided to pretend I didn't like that he'd snuck a peak.

"Well, Jackie Davenport, do you have any ID on you?" He arched a brow.

Shit. My shoulders sunk. I'd forgotten to put my wallet in my car before I'd left for my run. "I forgot it at home," I admitted with a little less attitude.

"Convenient." He shook his head to himself. "I think I'm gonna have to conduct a field sobriety test, given the amount of bottles littering the side of the road here," he said, tucking his thumbs into his belt and widening his stance.

He could not be serious. "Do I look like I'm out on a bender, Officer McTavish?" I motioned to my attire with both hands.

He raised a brow. "I'm not sure exactly what someone on a bender looks like to you, ma'am—"

I felt my blood pressure rising at his use of that damn word again.

"—but I can assure you that a half-dressed, red-faced, difficult woman doesn't exactly scream to me that she hasn't been drinking."

"I was jogging," I ground out.

He didn't answer me and instead walked a few paces to my car and lowered the trunk lid down. "Put your hands on the trunk please."

I dropped my hands to my side. "Are you arresting me?" I asked, dumbfounded.

"Relax. I'm going to pat you down to make sure you don't have anything I need to be concerned about and then I'm going to conduct the sobriety test."

Un-fucking-believable. This was unreal. Never in my life. I held my tongue as I stomped over to the trunk, faced it, and placed my palms on the hot metal.

"Is there anything on you I should know about? Any drugs, needles, paraphernalia?" he asked in a way that indicated he'd administered one of these on more than a few occasions.

"Of course not," I clipped.

He came to stand behind me. I couldn't see him, but his presence this close to me was like a magnet drawing me to him, and I found myself wanting to back up into his hard body.

He crouched down and why, oh why couldn't I get the image of him putting his face between my legs out of my head? Like I'd let this asshole touch me. When his hands circled my ankle, I sucked in a breath and fought the urge to bring my feet together to ease the ache in my center.

He slid his hands up my leg and I swore I heard a small groan escape his lips. My skin was tingling with awareness as his warm hands passed over me. Stopping short of the V of my thighs, he repeated the action on my other leg, moving just as slowly from the bottom to the top.

His hands then landed on my bare skin at my waist, and the sensation spread until it concentrated in my core. As his hands slid up to just below my breasts, I heard his breathing grow ragged behind me, and I had to fight the urge to press back into him.

Damn, what was wrong with me?

"Find what you're looking for, officer?" I asked with way more huskiness and way less ire than I'd intended.

He cleared his throat, and I heard his feet move away from me on the gravel. "You can turn around now."

I did what he asked and brought my hand to my waist, cocking a hip and an eyebrow. He appeared less together now than he had before he'd laid his hands on me. His face was flushed, and his hair looked like maybe he'd run his hands through it. Good, serves him right.

"Now, you're sure you've had nothing to drink." He cleared his throat, his gaze darting from my own for a second.

I rolled my eyes. "I already told you I didn't." I stepped forward until we were only inches apart. "Do you smell any alcohol on my breath?" I cocked my head back and sent a little thanks up to the Big Man that I'd finished

7

off a Certs in my car before the tire had blown. I blew a breath into his face, and he closed his eyes momentarily. It almost looked like he was savoring it.

After a second, his eyes snapped open. "Mind stepping back, ma'am?"

Anger had my entire body heating. I really might strangle him if he called me that one more time. I could already picture myself calling up my godfather, the Chief of Police, and confessing to murder later today.

Taking a step back, I waited for his instruction. I could introduce myself and tell him who I was. He'd certainly find out eventually—Bar Harbor and the surrounding area was not a big place. But at this point, he'd pissed me off and I'd rather let him make that discovery all on his own. Let him feel like the asshole he was when he did.

"Place your hands straight out and one at a time, alternating hands, touch your finger to your nose." He demonstrated exactly what it was he wanted, and I did what he asked without comment, just wanting to get this over and done with so I could be on my way, far removed from this infuriating yet somehow unbelievably attractive man.

"Great. Now say the alphabet for me start to finish." He placed both hands at his hips again, looking authoritative and serious, and, unfortunately for me, entirely fuckable. Damn him.

"A, b, c, d, e, f, g..." I sang until I'd gotten all the way through without any mishaps.

"You get extra points for actually singing it," he said and chuckled.

Wow, did Officer McTavish actually have a sense of humor? Interesting.

"Okay, seems everything is fine. You can relax." That was pretty much guaranteed not to happen with him around. "Would you like some help changing your tire?" His thumbs were hooked under his utility belt, and he nodded toward my other source of frustration.

As much as it begrudged me, I'd be an idiot to let him drive off while I still had no way to get the tire off. "I'd appreciate it." I didn't look at him when I responded. I had no interest in witnessing the smug smile I was sure was on his face.

He walked around me and bent down to grab the tire wrench. Sitting on his haunches, he worked silently as he went about getting the ruined tire off and putting the donut on. I was content to watch him unabashedly as his back and arm muscles tensed and relaxed while he worked.

When he was done, he straightened to his full height—which, if I had to guess, was over six feet—and held the tire wrench out to me. "Here, take this. I'll put the tire in your trunk." He did as he said, heaving it in, and then dusted off the front of his uniform.

I stepped beside him and placed the tire iron back in the trunk. "Thanks for helping me out." I brushed back a stray piece of hair that had escaped my ponytail.

"You should get the shop to look at that. Could be you just have a nail or something in it and they can patch it. Would save you having to buy a whole new tire." He smiled warmly at me and I couldn't help but return it with a smile of my own.

"I'll do that, thanks."

Jamie pointed to the evidence of my party girl ways on the shoulder. "You want some help putting those back in the vehicle?"

I shrugged. "I can handle it."

He smirked and I hated how it made his eyes sparkle just a bit. "Of course you can."

Keeping my face straight, we both stood awkwardly behind my car for a moment, not saying anything.

"Well…I'm gonna go," I finally said, fighting the internal pull that had me wanting to stay near him.

He nodded and began making his way back to his cruiser. "Be careful driving on that donut. Stay off any highways."

"Yes, officer." I did a mock salute.

He shook his head at me and laughed, sauntering back to his cruiser.

Smirking to myself as I got into my own car, I immediately started it up and cranked the air conditioning on full blast. I needed something to cool me off. Waiting until I could take a cold shower when I got home wasn't an option. Maybe he wasn't such a jerk. He'd been much nicer at the end of our encounter and he had changed my tire for me.

Making sure the doors were unlocked, I stepped out and over to the pile of empties and began returning them to my trunk. By the time I'd finished, I was more than aware that Jamie was probably leering at me from inside his cruiser. Because he was still there, in his car, idling. I had tried really hard not to stick my ass out more than necessary when I was leaning in to place the boxes down, but it was like the thing had a mind of its own, I swear.

Straightening up, I slammed the trunk closed and walked to the driver's side with a little extra swing in my hips. I didn't turn to glance at him. No way was I going to give him the satisfaction. When I slumped down into my seat, I sighed at the cool jets of air streaming across my overheated skin, then leaned my head back and closed my eyes, exhaling a long breath. I needed a minute to cool down—both from the weather and from Jamie.

I'd just decided to head home when a knock on the glass startled me so much I nearly jumped from my seat. It was Jamie, bent over so that his face was flush with mine. I hit the button to roll down the window.

"Yes?" I asked, irritation once again ringing through in my tone.

He shoved a piece of paper at me. "Your taillight is out. Need to get that fixed."

I grabbed the piece of paper from him and glanced down to realize that the bastard had given me a ticket. "What the hell!" I turned to give him a piece of my mind, but he was already halfway back to his cruiser. Spying him through my mirror, I let a cry of frustration out.

"Arrr!" That was it! I was out of here! Smacking the steering wheel, I put the car in gear and drove off, happy to leave the infuriating man that was Jamie McTavish behind me.

# *Chapter Two*

## JAMIE

I entered the station hours later, still trying to get Jackie out of my head—the one between my shoulders *and* the one between my legs. That running gear she'd been sporting should've been illegal. The vision of her toned body in that tight-clinging fabric was now seared into my brain. I'd been adjusting myself all afternoon as a result.

When she'd been all up on me trying to prove she hadn't been drinking and then growled? Fuck me. You could've hung a ten pound weight off my dick it was so hard.

With a sigh, I shoved some stuff in my locker and decided to stop at my buddy, Ben's, desk to see if he wanted to go out for a beer later. He was a detective on the force and one of the first people I'd become friends with when I'd moved to town.

He looked up from his desk as I approached, the gel in his slicked back dark hair reflecting the florescent lights above. "I hear you had an interesting day," he said with a Cheshire-like grin on his face.

What the hell was he talking about? I shrugged. "How so?"

"Heard you had a run-in with Jackie."

My back went ramrod straight wondering how he knew Jackie and exactly how well. "You know her?" I arched an eyebrow.

"We all know her around here." He motioned with his hands around the station.

Did Jackie get around like that? She'd seemed like she had an unpredictable side, but somehow I couldn't picture her sleeping around.

"What do you mean?" I asked with more force than I should have.

"She's a nine-one-one operator. Grew up in Bar Harbor, and she's the chief's goddaughter..." he pinned me with an intense look. "You'll see when you've been here a while longer. You'll run into her often."

My stomach sank as I blew out a breath and ran a hand through my hair. For fuck's sake. "Wish I'd known that earlier," I grumbled.

"What'd you do?" His expression became serious.

"She was at the side of the road with a flat and a shit-ton of empties from her car on the shoulder." I grimaced. "I may have patted her down, gave her a sobriety test, and a ticket for her taillight being out."

Ben laughed. "You did not." He leaned back in his chair, holding his stomach while he laughed so hard that tears leaked from his eyes. "Oh, I bet she didn't like that at all, did she?"

"Not so much." I pressed my lips together.

"Oh, man. I would've loved to have seen that." He was still laughing and finally stopped to catch his breath. "She didn't tell you who she was?"

I shook my head. "I'm thinking now that she was leaving that for me to find out on my own and feel like an ass about it." I massaged my temples with my hands.

"Wait until the rest of the guys find out about this." He wiped at the tears that had escaped his eyes.

"Piss off, man." I pressed my lips together.

"So, what did you think of her?" he asked, raising a brow.

I narrowed my eyes. "What do you mean?"

He grinned knowingly at me. "You know exactly what I mean."

I shrugged, trying to play it off like she wasn't the most stunning female I'd seen in years...my whole life maybe. "She was a little prickly, but I can see what the appeal might be."

Ben smacked his hand down on the desk and shook his head. "He can see what the appeal might be," he said to himself, amused. When he was done laughing at my expense, he added, "Don't waste your time. She doesn't date cops."

"Who said anything about dating her?" I had something in mind, that's for sure, but I wasn't sure it was dating.

"Believe me, I've seen more than one new guy come into this division and set their sights on her. They're always disappointed."

I took a step closer to his desk and lowered my voice. Now I was intrigued. "Why won't she date a cop?"

He shrugged. "Don't know. But many have tried and failed before you, my friend."

I wonder what that was about. Like was it a hard and fast rule, or had she just not had any use for any of the other guys that had tried? "Whatever, man. Pretty sure I'm on her shit list now anyway."

"Oh, you can be sure you are."

I rolled my eyes. "You wanna get a beer later on?"

"Yeah, sure. The ball game's on tonight. I'm just wrapping up here. I'll meet you at the bar in a few."

I nodded. "Sounds good." I turned and walked away, then stopped when something dawned on me. "Hey, how did you know I'd run into her?"

He gave a low chuckle and glanced back down to the mountain of papers on his desk. "You ran her plates. Word travels fast."

Apparently it did. I'd have to keep in mind that I wasn't in the big city anymore.

# Chapter Three

## Jackie

I headed up to Don and Shawna's house, carrying the Greek salad I'd made, careful not to spill any. Given the surprise nature of the party tonight, I had parked around the corner. I was here to celebrate the retirement of my pseudo father, Don. He'd been a cop for more than thirty-five years and had been my dad's former partner. He'd acted as the chief for the last several years and was due to retire next week. Shawna had retired a few years earlier and I know she'd been looking forward to Don joining her. She'd been busy making plans for all the travelling she wanted to do.

The feeling was bittersweet as I knocked on the door. I should've been able to do this for my father, too. He and Don should've been retiring together, but that had been ripped away from me when I was ten. I swallowed past the lump in my throat as I tried picturing what he might look like if he was still alive today.

I blinked away tears as Shawna swung the door open with a big smile. "Jackie, I'm so glad to see you. Can you believe this day is finally here?"

I smiled and leaned in for a hug, moving the bowl off to my side. "I know. I wouldn't miss this for anything. I'm so excited for you both."

Shawna brushed some hair off my forehead, her smile turning strained. "I know, sweetie. Don will be glad to see you, too." She moved away from the door, allowing me entry.

As I stepped in, I noticed the gleaming old hardwood floors and patterned wallpaper. The place looked the same as ever. After my father had been killed, Don had stepped in as a sort of makeshift father. I'd spent a lot of time in his house growing up, but not so much lately. I suppose that was just how it was as anyone transitioned into adulthood. I didn't see my mom as much as I should anymore either.

As I made my way down the hall to the back of the house, chit-chatting with Shawna about what was new, the rumble of voices grew louder. We entered the kitchen and through the glass doors in the breakfast area, I saw that everyone else was outside in the backyard. Some were lounging on patio chairs, while others congregated around the yard, beers in hand. A few were sitting along the edge of the pool, dipping their legs in.

I surveyed the crowd, realizing I knew almost all of them. The odd wife dotted the landscape of the mostly male assembly. There were firemen, cops, and EMTs.

"Where do you want me to put this?" I asked Shawna.

She scrunched her lips to one side. "The fridge up here is already full, and I don't want to leave it out in the heat. Why don't you see if you can find some room in the fridge downstairs? Don added a beer fridge to the wine cellar." Shawna rolled her eyes, obviously not impressed with his addition.

I chuckled. "Alright. Be right back." I walked back

toward the front of the house until I reached the basement door under the main staircase. Propping the bowl on my hip so I'd have a free hand, I turned the handle and swung the door open, starting down the stairs.

When I reached the bottom, I headed to the area below the basement stairs where the wine cellar was and placed the bowl inside the fridge at the back of the small room.

As I headed up again, Shawna was at the top of the stairs. "Find a place for it?"

"Yep. We're all good."

"Excellent. Now get out there and grab a drink from one of the coolers and enjoy yourself. Don should be home in about half an hour. I can't wait to see his face when he sees everyone."

Feeling excited for my godfather and looking forward to having a good time seeing everyone, I slid the glass door open and headed into the backyard. The heat was like walking into a wall, and I was thankful I'd chosen my spaghetti strapped sun dress, rather than shorts and a T-shirt.

I said hello to some people I knew and found one of the coolers on the corner of the stone patio. Spotting one of my favorite beers inside, I pushed my hand into the icy cold water. As I was pulling the bottle out, I heard a voice behind me.

"I'd recognize that ass anywhere."

My entire body froze, all my muscles tensing. I knew that voice. I straightened up and turned around to find Jamie behind me. I narrowed my eyes. "What did you just say?"

"Pretty sure you heard me," he responded with a cocky grin.

My mouth went slack-jawed when Shawna came up beside me. "Jackie, I see you've met Jamie. He's only been in town a few months. Came to us by way of Boston."

I sucked in a big breath, attempting to lower my quickly rising blood pressure. "Yes, we've met." I wasn't about to ruin Don's party by spouting off to Jamie in front of the hostess just because I didn't like his newest addition to the team.

Shawna went on, not noticing the irritation I was trying very hard to conceal. "Jamie, Jackie is our goddaughter. She's very special to Don. He's got a soft spot in his heart for this one." Shawna put her arm around me for a second and squeezed me into her.

Jamie's eyes widened for a moment. I could only hope it was in fear.

"I'd heard that," he said, nodding and tipping back his beer.

Shawna smiled. "She's like family to us, this one. Did you know she's a nine-one-one operator?"

I was beginning to get the feeling that maybe she was talking me up in hopes that he'd like me. I mentally rolled my eyes. Shawna was always harping on me to settle down. Not happening. I enjoyed my freedom.

Jamie took another sip of his beer, his gaze holding steady on my face the whole time. "I did hear that, yes."

Shawna leaned into me and in a conspiratorial whisper said, "Don's actually quite fond of Jamie, too. Thinks he has a bright future ahead of him."

I pursed my lips together and nodded. Great. Now I *had* to play nice with him. I had too much respect for Don to do otherwise.

"Well, I'll leave you kids to talk. I want to keep a look out for Don so we can be sure to surprise him." Shawna clapped her hands in front of her in an excited gesture and walked away.

I tried to twist the cap off of my bottle, but it wouldn't budge, the sharp edges on the cap only digging into my fingers instead. I blew out a frustrated breath.

"Here let me." Jamie set his beer down on the patio table beside us and held his hand out. Begrudgingly, I handed it over. He brought it up to this mouth, clamped his teeth around it, and turned the beer bottle. He pulled the bottle away from his mouth, the top remaining between his teeth.

"Doesn't that hurt?" I asked, one-half appalled the other half slightly turned on.

He shrugged, handing my beer back to me and picking up his own. "Something I learned in college."

"Good to see all that money was put to good use," I said with sarcasm. I lifted the bottle to my lips, and suddenly all I could focus on was the fact that this bottle had been in his mouth. Even if only a little.

Without warning, desire raced through my bloodstream as I considered what it would be like to kiss him. It wasn't that hard to imagine, really. He looked good tonight. I'd thought he was hot in his uniform, but damn, he was even more attractive in regular clothes. He was wearing a pair of cargo shorts and a button down shirt with a plaid pattern. His muscular arms were practically bulging from underneath, and there was something so boyish and appealing about the way his hair curled up at the back over top of his collar. I found myself wanting to touch it. Wanting to touch him.

Jamie pressed his lips together, looking contrite. "Listen, I want to apologize about what went down when we first met. I didn't know who you were. I'm sorry."

I was surprised to get an apology from him and, though I appreciated it, I wasn't letting him off that easy. I crossed my arms over my chest. "You were obnoxious."

"I was doing my job," he said in a placating tone.

"Does your job involve frisking women in little to no clothing?" I raised a brow.

"That's one of the perks, actually." He smirked at me. I arched a brow and said nothing when he sighed. "In all seriousness, if I think a woman might've been drinking and driving, yeah, I do what I have to." When I didn't respond again, he continued, "Oh, come on. You have to admit there were a lot of empties on the side of that road."

I gritted my teeth. Why did this guy grate on me so much? I didn't want to do this, even though I was equal parts irritated and turned on, which was a new dynamic for me.

Eager to get away, I noticed one of the guys I had tried setting Chloe up with at the party that had led to all the empties on the other side of the road.

With a tight smile, I told him, "If you'll excuse me, there's someone I'd like to go talk to."

I brushed past him, not waiting for a reply and careful not to make contact. The last thing I needed was for my body to be even more heated than it already was.

# *Chapter Four*

## JAMIE

Jesus Christ, was she trying to kill me? I'd been here for hours and as if the sight of Jackie in her cute sundress wasn't enough, I'd had to spend the past hour watching her bounce around the pool while a group played volleyball. The chocolate brown bikini she was wearing clung to her firm figure and left little to the imagination. She'd pulled her dark hair up into a messy bun and the green in her eyes seemed even more prominent than usual because of the sun she'd gotten on her face earlier.

"Jamie, why don't you join us?" Ben yelled across to me from the pool. "Patterson has to get back to the Mrs., and we need someone to sub in."

I'd brought my suit since the invite referred to the event as a retirement/pool party. Getting a closer view of Jackie in that flimsy scrap of fabric she called a swimsuit wouldn't hurt either.

"Give me a minute, and I'll go change," I shouted back.

Jackie's lips formed a thin line, as if she didn't approve of my joining their little game, which only made it that much sweeter for me. The sexual tension that had been thrumming between us had me wanting to get under her skin. I figured if I couldn't touch it, I could get under it at the very least.

But by the time I made my way over to the pool, the game had changed and the guys were now playing with the women hoisted up on their shoulders. I felt a grin forming on my face. This ought to be fun. My gut tightened when I saw Jackie's tanned legs wrapped around the shoulders of the guy she'd left me to go speak to earlier. They certainly seemed cozy with one another. What was the deal with those two?

I mentally shook it off. I had no claim to her. Jackie could do what she wanted. As could I.

I politely pushed my way through the crowd on the patio area and caught Jackie's eye a moment before I reached the pool. I grinned with satisfaction when I noticed her gaze dart down the expanse of my chest and back up. When she caught me looking at her perusal of my assets, her eyes flared for a second and then morphed into an expression that reminded me of a child who'd been caught doing something wrong.

I chuckled and dove into the pool. "Okay, what are we playing?" I asked once I surfaced.

"Jamie, you get Sylvia on your shoulders," Ben said.

I glanced over at the blond waiting in the corner of the pool. She gave me a coy smile. I didn't know who Sylvia was, but I smiled warmly and introduced myself.

"I'm Jamie. Good to meet you." I held my hand out for her.

She giggled for a second, then shook it. "Sylvia, pleasure. I'm glad you decided to join us."

Someone made a disgusted sound behind me. "Are you guys going to ogle each other all afternoon or are we going to play?" It was Jackie, and she sounded irritated. If I didn't know better, I would've guessed jealous.

I turned to face her, almost laughing. She looked pouty with her hands crossed over her chest and a scowl on her face.

"Hold up there, princess. Give us a minute." I grinned, knowing my comment would antagonize her further.

She made another sound of frustration and uncrossed her arms.

"You ready to kick their ass?" I asked Sylvia.

"Definitely!" She flipped her platinum hair behind her shoulder and smiled.

I swam down under the water where Sylvia had widened her stance and put my head between her legs, rising up out of the water so that her thighs rested on my shoulders. When I came up out of the water, I saw Jackie bending down as best she could and whispering into her partner's ear. The guy whose shoulders she was on patted her leg and nodded. My jaw clenched at the sight of his hand on her thigh.

"Alright. Three points until match. You all set?" the guy who was acting as referee shouted.

Everyone on both sides nodded, and I spread apart from my other teammates to cover the most ground. As I watched the muscles in Jackie's thighs clench around the other guy's neck, I vowed that I, too, would have my head between Jackie's legs before the night was over.

This wasn't exactly what I'd had in mind, I thought as I heaved Jackie onto my shoulders and rose out of the water. After my team had dominated the past two games, Ben had suggested mixing the players up, and he'd ever so helpfully suggested that Jackie and I be partners. I couldn't decide if he was an asshole or a god for it because now I was sporting a raging hard-on below water level, while Jackie's firm thighs gripped my neck and her pussy pushed into the back of my head. It was both a dream and a fucking nightmare.

"Your serve," Jackie called to the other team from above me.

The three couples on the other side spread out, and the couple serving shot the ball in our direction. I bounded to the right. Not easy to do with an erect dick between my legs, but I was just in time for Jackie to bump the ball back to the other side.

"Good shot," I hollered and patted her calf. The muscles tensed under her warm skin at my touch, drawing her thighs closer around my head.

"Thanks," she said in a clipped tone.

We played the rest of the game without any more incidents of sexual tension—both of our competitive sides rising to the surface. Twenty minutes later and our side had won by three points. We made a pretty good team actually. When she wasn't trying to brush me off, that is.

Jackie squirmed on top of my shoulders. "You can let me down now."

That little action got things moving again below water level. "Your wish is my command, princess." I let my legs fall out from under me and dropped into the water, taking Jackie with me.

We both rose up at the same time, Jackie sputtering. I grinned wide.

"You jerk!" She shoved me with one hand, but barely moved me. I grabbed her wrist, and laughed along with everyone else who'd witnessed my prank. Her pulse beat frantically under my touch and after the laughter died away, we stared at each other, both of us breathing heavily—something passed between us, something I didn't know how to quantify.

"I'm sorry. I was just joking around." I let her hand drop.

"No, it's fine." She glanced down at her hands. "I overreacted." Without another word or even glancing at me again, she swam to the stairs and exited the pool. I would've followed her—wished I could—but until this fucking hard-on had subsided, I'd be staying put.

ELISABETH GRACE

# Chapter Five

## Jackie

Evening was approaching and the intensity of the sun was dying down. A few people were still hanging out in the pool, but the majority were lounging around the patio. The radio played in the background and the scent of suntan lotion and the burgers cooking on the barbeque was in the air.

"I think I'm going to start putting some of the food out on the table now that the sun has dipped below the trees. Jackie, do mind grabbing the salad you brought?" Shawna asked me.

"Not at all." I set my beer down on the table and pulled my towel off the back of the chair, patting down my legs to make sure they weren't still wet. I didn't think Shawna would appreciate me tracking water through her house. I reached into my bag, which hung off the chair, and pulled my cover up out, tugging the thin fabric over my head.

Inside, I made my way down to the basement. It was cooler down here than upstairs and a small chill stole over my skin, pebbling my nipples underneath my triangle bikini top. I pulled the heavy wood door underneath the stairs open and entered the wine cellar. The walls were lined with custom shelving, filled top to bottom with an assortment of different wine bottles, the scent of the cedar heavy in the air.

I stopped short.

Jamie? What the hell was he doing in here?

"You following me, hot stuff?" he said with a practiced smile.

"Of course not! I just came to get my salad from the fridge. What're you doing here?" I propped my hands on my hips, irritated once again to be forced into such close proximity to him.

"Same." He nodded toward the fridge he was holding open. "I brought some dip." He closed the door and leaned against it with his arms crossed over his chest. The way his muscles bunched drew my eyes to them. He pushed up and stalked toward me.

It wasn't warm in here, but I suddenly felt like I was overheating, as if I was still out in the summer sun. As he moved closer, I backed up into one of the shelves, the tops of the bottles pressing into my back.

Finally, he came to a stop mere inches away. "Don't you think it's about time we addressed whatever's going on between us?"

I guffawed. "There's nothing going on between us."

His gray eyes narrowed. "That's bullshit and you know it. Why would you follow me in here otherwise?" Reaching out, he ran a finger down from the base of my throat, dragging it slowly over my heated skin to the juncture of my cleavage, then let his hand drop.

I didn't stop him. *Why didn't I stop him?*

I suppressed a small shiver and fought the urge to close my eyes, instead pinning him with a glare. "What do you think you're doing?" Damn it. That sounded way huskier than I'd intended.

"What you want me to," he said, full of confidence.

My face tightened and I pressed my lips together before responding. "I want no such thing." I pushed by him, forgetting all about the salad. I was only steps from the door when Jamie reached for my waist and tugged me toward him so that my back was pressed against his muscled chest.

"Let. Me. Go," I ground out, using the anger I felt at myself for liking the way I fit into his body, against him.

"When are you going to acknowledge that you feel it, too?" his husky voice said into my ear.

My hair was still pulled up so I felt every word with his warm breath against my neck. "The only thing I feel for you is frustration." I wriggled against his grip, but he had a firm hold of me.

"Is that right." He chuckled. "Well, I actually believe you when you say I frustrate you."

"Good. Now let me go." I tried keeping the irate tone to my voice, but being encased in his arms was weakening my resolve.

To my surprise, he unwrapped his arms and moved back slightly, but before I could react or book it out of there, Jamie's hands went to the hem of my cover-up and in one fell swoop he lifted it over my head.

I started to spin around to cuss him out, but his large hands pulled me toward him so my back was once again pressed against his chest.

"I think your frustration with me is *all* sexual, though." He dragged the side of his face along mine, nuzzling me like a pet would. "Why don't we see if I can take care of some of that for you?" he whispered into my ear.

I closed my eyes and leaned my head back onto his shoulder, unable to keep at bay all the elicit images his words were bringing to mind.

I'd had my share of men and no one had ever affected me even close to the way Jamie did. I didn't sleep around for sport, but I was young and carefree. I enjoyed having fun and if I was dating a guy and was attracted to him, I wasn't going to stay celibate just because of some inane moral obligation. I didn't do emotional entanglements, so over the years I'd dated a lot of guys.

I was always the one who had the upper hand. Always. Because I didn't get emotionally invested, and it didn't matter to me what happened between me and the guy I was seeing. And yet, somehow I knew Jamie had the potential to change the dynamic I was accustomed to.

I couldn't let that happen. I wouldn't.

"That's it, baby." He pressed closer to me, the sensation of his skin against my almost naked back causing a small moan to escape my mouth. "Put your hands behind my neck. You move them and I stop."

One of his hands moved ever so slowly up to my breast, pulling aside the bikini top to play with my nipple. My sex clenched as he twisted and rolled it between his thumb and forefinger.

"You have a beautiful body, Jackie. Never cover it up around me." His voice was deep and soaked in sex.

I had a fleeting thought of telling him that whatever was about to happen here was a one-time thing, that I wasn't his, but it fell from my mind as his other hand dipped into my bikini bottom.

"Put your left foot up on the shelf."

I did as he asked, without hesitation, wantonly opening myself to him and allowing his fingers better access. And was I ever glad I did.

"How come you didn't take instruction this well the first time we met?" He gave a low chuckle.

I had a witty comeback on the tip of my tongue, but just then his right hand dipped lower, his fingers brushing over my clit and rimming the entrance to my sex, but not entering. I moaned and squirmed against his fingers.

"Oh Jackie, I'd love to, but the first part of me inside you is going to be either my tongue or my cock. I haven't decided which. For today you'll have to just deal with my attention here." He punctuated his last word with a swirl over top of my swollen bud. I arched back into him, unable to stop my reaction.

His left hand pinched my nipple, while his right lavished attention on my clit. Again and again he kept up this pattern until I was a panting, quivering mess.

"God, you smell so fucking good, Jackie. Do you know how hard it makes me, being able to smell how turned on you are?" He pushed his groin into my lower back so I could feel his rigid length.

A small cry escaped my lips, and I couldn't help but pull the hair on the back of his head where my hands rested.

"Ah, my kitten wants to finish, does she? You're pretty amenable when you retract your claws long enough to let me get my hands on you. Lucky for you, I aim to please." He nuzzled his face into my neck and continued fondling me, playing with me, driving me to the edge. My knees shook slightly as I gazed down at my body and saw for myself what his skilled hands were doing.

Heat pooled at the apex of my thighs as the need to come built up to a peak, then Jamie dragged his tongue from the base of my neck up to my earlobe where his teeth bit down and I came apart. White light bathed my vision while I moaned, squeezing my eyes shut and shuddering in his arms. I had the fleeting thought that someone might hear, but as I slipped further and further into sensation it disappeared.

As I came back to earth, I slunk down to the cool floor, leaning against Jamie as I did. That orgasm had been mind-numbing, but I couldn't look up at him. Somehow I knew I'd only see a smug, satisfied smile on his handsome face.

I righted my bikini top, reached for my cover-up that lay in front of me. I pushed up off the cool ceramic floor and raced out of that wine cellar without a word or a backward glance.

# Chapter Six

## Jackie

I managed to avoid Jamie for the rest of the party, though I knew he was watching me. I could practically feel his eyes on me. He didn't stay long after our wine cellar rendezvous and left without a goodbye, which had irked me. And the fact that it irked me, irked me even more. There was no reason it should matter, but I found myself drinking more than I normally would in an effort to try and forget about him and what he'd done to me in that basement.

After paying the cab driver and stumbling into my house, I pulled my cell phone from my purse and sifted through my contacts for my best friend. After several rings, she answered. It was clear I'd woken her, based on the groggy sound to her voice.

"Chloeeeeee," I whined into my cell.

I heard her yawn into the phone. "Jackie, what time is it?"

"I didn't look. This is a girlfriend emergency."

"Are you drunk?" There was a slight tone of disapproval to her voice.

"I'm fairly tipsy, not drunk," I said a little too defensively.

"I'd love to know the distinction someday." She laughed.

"I'm serious, Chlo. I need you. I did something really stupid tonight."

She sighed. "Uh-oh. This must be really bad if my live-in-the-moment friend is this freaked about it. What happened?"

I plopped down onto the chair in my living room, hanging my legs over one armrest and leaning my head on the other. "You remember that cop I told you ticketed me?"

"Uh, yeah. You complained about what an asshat he was for like a day straight."

"He was at the party." I draped my arm over my eyes.

"Please tell me you didn't actually rip his balls off and feed them to him like you so vividly described last week."

"Har-har. No I did not. Though it does kinda have to do with his balls...in a round-about way." Chloe said nothing, silently waiting for an explanation. "The long and short of it is we fooled around."

Chloe laughed at my expense. "Well?"

"Well, what?" I said with a huff.

"Was it long or short?"

Clearly my so-called best friend wasn't seeing the seriousness of this situation. "I don't know," I said, flustered. "Based upon the feel of it pressing against me I'd say the latter."

"Wait. What exactly happened?"

"He ambushed me in Don and Shawna's wine cellar and got me off." I blew out a breath. I can't believe I'd gone through with it. I mean I was no nun, but I didn't even know the guy.

"I don't understand why you sound so foul then. Seems like you had a pretty good time at the party." She was way too amused for my liking.

"I don't want to like this guy," I argued, gazing up at the ceiling above me. Well the parts that weren't starting to spin anyway. "First of all, he's a cop and you know how I feel about that—"

"I do know how you feel about it," she interrupted, "and I know *you* know how I feel about that."

I pulled my arm up and rolled my eyes. This was a subject we'd never see eye-to-eye on. She couldn't understand how I chose to work surrounded by emergency service workers, how I had the utmost respect for them, and yet I refused to consider dating one. But she wasn't the one who had lost her father to the job when she was ten.

"Anyway," I went on, stretching out the word in a moody way, "He was a complete pompous ass the first time I met him, and he acts like it's a foregone conclusion that we're going to sleep together."

Chloe chuckled. "Gee, I wonder what gave him that idea."

"I'm serious," I whined again. "Now he's going to think he can snap his fingers, and I'll come running, legs wide open."

Another chuckle. "What did he say after?"

I huffed into the phone. "I didn't give him the chance. I ran out of there and avoided him the rest of the party. I felt him watching me the whole time, though." His steel gray eyes might as well have been branding me.

"Now you just sound dramatic," she sighed.

"Trust me. When this guy looks at you—you feel it. Everywhere." A full body shiver wracked through my body just remembering how heated I'd felt whenever his eyes were on me.

"You obviously like him," Chloe reasoned. "What's the harm in spending some time with him and seeing where it goes?"

I went rigid in the chair. "You know I don't do emotional entanglements, Chlo. And I'm certainly not going to break my rules for a cop. I'm *not* going to end up like my mother." It sounded harsh, but I couldn't stomach the idea of turning into her. I loved my mom, but from the moment my dad had been killed in the line of duty, she'd been mourning a ghost. She'd never moved on with her life, and never dated or loved anyone else in the sixteen years since. No one else could compare to the memory of my dad in her mind.

"Then I guess you'll have to avoid him," Chloe said, matter of fact. "You obviously can't control yourself around him."

I groaned. "How am I supposed to stay away from him when I know it's that good when he lays his hands on me? Can you imagine what the sex would be like?"

"Sounds like quite the dilemma." She laughed.

"I'm damned if I do and damned if I don't," I whined again, feeling my frustration mounting.

Chloe yawned into the phone, and I suddenly remembered what time it was. "Shit. I'm sorry I called so late. I'll let you go."

"Sorry, I was up early this morning to take Jess to work." Chloe was the sole caregiver for her teenage sister.

"No worries. I'll call you in the morning. Any chance you can run me over to Don's to pick up my car? I had to take a cab home."

"Of course. Give me a call and we'll head over."

"Alright. Thanks for always having my back and dealing with my fucked up issues. Love you, babe."

"Same here. Night."

I let my phone fall in my lap. I lay there for a while and pictured Jamie with no shirt on. The way his abdominal muscles rippled when he moved, how his biceps flexed when he'd lob the ball across the pool, had been mouthwatering. And then I fell asleep, dreaming of his large hands on me, groping, teasing, and bringing me to climax before I woke up on the chair with a crick in my neck and managed to drag my ass to bed for a fitful sleep.

ELISABETH GRACE

## *Chapter Seven*

# JAMIE

I pulled the cruiser into Jackie's driveway. What the hell was wrong with me? It was only yesterday that I'd gotten her off and yet here I was, sitting unannounced in her driveway like a fucking stalker.

If I'd thought it difficult to get her off my mind before, what had happened in the wine cellar had made it damn near impossible. I'd ended up going home and jacking off, then taking a cold shower, but the feel of her slick heat and the smell of her arousal still taunted my mind.

Everyone I'd talked to had said the same thing— that she'd turned down each and every cop or fireman that had asked her out. No one was sure if she was just trying to keep her personal life outside of the work environment or what, but I intended to find out. The insane pull between us didn't leave me any other choice.

With a sigh, I unbuckled my seatbelt and glanced at the small bungalow. It was cute with white siding and black shutters. Hanging baskets of colorful flowers hung from hooks around the veranda and a kickass bicycle was leaning against the side of the house. That helped to explain why she had such a firm ass.

I opened the door to the cruiser when the front door of the house burst open, and Jackie stood there frozen, her hand held to her chest and such an expression of fear on her face that I bolted out of the car and up the front steps.

"What's wrong?" I demanded as soon as I was in front of her.

"Wh-what are you doing here?" she asked in barely a whisper.

I relaxed a fraction once it was clear she was okay. "I figured you could use a lift to Don's place for your car. Didn't think you would've driven home last night." I shrugged. "It's been quiet today, so I popped by to see if you wanted me to drive you over."

She released a pent-up breath and relief washed over her face. "Oh, thank God."

I frowned and gripped her upper arms. "What's going on? Everything okay?"

She glanced down at where my hands lay on her soft skin and looked back up to me, blinking twice. "It's nothing. When I saw the cruiser in the driveway...never mind." She shook her head.

I studied her for a moment. She was sexy just rolling out of bed with her hair thrown in a messy bun and last night's make-up still on her face. "You sure?"

She nodded and her eyes flicked down to my hands once more. "Why are you always touching me whenever I see you?" Her voice had come out all breathy, not at all convincing me that she didn't like my hands right where they were.

I grazed her collarbones with my thumbs, causing goose bumps to form on her skin. "I think you know exactly why."

With a gulp, she stepped back and I released her, dropping my hands to my sides. Her eyes narrowed the tiniest bit—something I'd learned meant she was beginning to get annoyed with me, and I had to ask her again. "Are you telling me you haven't felt this pull since the moment we met?"

Jackie sucked her bottom lip into her mouth. God, what I wouldn't do to be able to suck on that lip right now. I reached forward and pulled her lip down so it popped out of her mouth.

She just stared up at me for a moment, unblinking. "You're certainly not the first guy I've been attracted to, Jamie." She crossed her arms over her chest, trying, I think, to show her displeasure. Unfortunately for her, all it did was advertise the fact that her nipples were hard.

I stepped closer, wanting to make her a little uncomfortable, and force her to confront the issue at hand. "It's more than that, and you know it."

"Pfft. Don't flatter yourself." She rolled her eyes.

I leaned down into the crook of her neck. Her scent was clean and fresh, with a slight citrus tinge to it. I spoke slowly into her ear. "Your body betrays you, Jackie. Your nipples are hard, your breath is more shallow than when I first arrived. The body doesn't lie, but you do."

She inhaled a sharp breath, and then pressed both her hands against my chest to push me away. "You need to leave." Her face was blotchy.

I chuckled, loving the affect I had on her. Why couldn't she just admit it, and then we could skip all this bullshit and get to the good stuff. "What about your car?"

She turned her head to the side, tucking a stray piece of dark hair behind her ear. "I have a friend coming to get me. It's not your concern."

I clenched my fists at my side, wondering if it was

that jackass from yesterday. "This wouldn't be the same 'friend' who had you on his shoulders yesterday in the pool, would it?"

Her face scrunched up. "Jared? Not that it's any of your business, I love Jared, but we're just friends. Besides, I was on your shoulders yesterday, too, and I don't even like you." She raised her chin and placed her hands on her hips like she'd just shot the winning lob my way.

I narrowed my eyes ever so slightly. "Keep telling yourself that, sweetheart, but I'm pretty sure it was me who had you half-naked and panting yesterday, not him."

Her lips twisted in disapproval. "Argh! Go! Just get out of here."

I had to bite down to keep from laughing. She really was pretty fucking hot when she was pissed. Maybe that was why I enjoyed riling her up so much.

"One date, Jackie," I said, totally serious. "That's what I want. It's not like I'm down on bended knee."

Her hand shot out in front of her, and she shoved me again, this time forcing me backward. "I'm not going out with you, so you might as well stop asking," she growled.

I stopped moving when she'd just about pushed me down her front steps. "Yeah, I heard you don't date cops. Why is that again?" I arched a brow.

"None of your business. Now go! I have to get ready before Chloe gets here."

I was ashamed to admit to the small amount of relief I felt at knowing it was another female who was coming to help Jackie collect her car. "Fine. This isn't over though." I slid my sunglasses onto my face. "You can't ignore this...*thing* between us forever." At that, I turned, taking the stairs down her porch.

"How did you find out where I live?" she shouted at me when I'd almost reached the car.

I opened my door and leaned one hand on the roof, facing her. "I'm a cop, Jackie. There's not much I can't find out about you if I want to." I winked and got into the cruiser and put my seatbelt on. When I looked up, she had already gone back into the house.

I smacked my hand on the steering wheel. Damn, that woman was frustrating. Why did she fight the inevitable? Because one thing was for certain—I wasn't about to let Jackie slip through my grasp. I'd have her one way or another.

ELISABETH GRACE

# *Chapter Eight*

## *Jackie*

After a couple of weeks had gone by, I'd managed to forget almost all about Jamie. Well, that wasn't entirely true. I'd been keeping myself as busy as possible, dividing my time between work, my fitness regime, and hanging out with Chloe. But at night, when I was alone with my thoughts and by myself in bed, my vibrator had been getting quite a workout.

I was desperate. So much so that when Brad asked me out I agreed. Anything to get rid of the image of Jamie's hands on me.

Brad wasn't typically my type. He was more straight-laced than I was used to, probably more uptight than I'd ever be comfortable with, but I figured what the hell. He worked at the bank, and I'd ran into him a few times. I was young (if you could call twenty-six still young), single, and it was better than sitting around on a Friday night, getting off with a poor imitation of the real thing, while daydreaming about a guy I wouldn't have.

Knowing that this date probably wasn't going to go

anywhere, I had opted to meet Brad at the Cottage Street Pub for drinks, a tiny bar just off Main Street which meant less tourists. It would also help to avoid the inevitable awkward goodbye at my doorstep later.

It was easy to spot Brad at the corner of the bar when I walked in, given the small size of the place. He smiled and waved to me as I approached.

He looked handsome in a nice guy sort-of way with his hair trimmed close to his scalp and his dress shirt tucked into his khaki pants.

I hadn't wanted to make a huge effort, so I'd opted for a pair of mint green skinny jeans, a white and tan striped tank, with a short white blazer over top. By the look on Brad's face, he approved.

I smiled when I reached him and placed my purse down on the bar in front of me. "Hi, Brad."

"You look wonderful tonight." His gaze raked over me.

"Thanks." I felt a little awkward accepting the compliment from him for some reason. Probably because my subconscious knew I really wanted it to be someone else complimenting me.

"What can I get you to drink?" he asked rather eagerly.

"A wine spritzer would be great. I'm driving." I crossed my legs and rested my hands on my knee. Somewhat awkward on a bar stool which suited since awkward was how I was feeling in his presence.

"Coming right up." He motioned for the bartender, ordered my drink, and then turned to face me. "Thanks for agreeing to this." He ran a hand through his blond hair in a nervous gesture, then adjusted his wire-framed glasses.

"You don't have to thank me, Brad." I gave him a forced smile.

The bartender returned and placed my spritzer

down in front of me. I thanked him and then took a sip. It was a shame I couldn't drink more. I had a feeling I was going to need it. Nothing about this date felt right—not at all how I felt when I was around Jamie. It was going to be a long night.

An hour later, my eyes were glazing over as Brad continued droning on about interest rates and annuities, none of which I found even remotely interesting. I wasn't sure whether he was nervous and that's why he kept going on and on or what. I was pretty sure it was evident that I wasn't on the edge of my seat.

As Brad started to delve into a story about a woman who'd come into the bank last week looking for a refinance on a house that wasn't even hers, laughter erupted behind us from some people who sounded like they'd just walked in the door.

There was nothing remarkable about that, but when the laughter stopped and someone in the small group spoke up from behind me, my back went ramrod straight, all my muscles tensing. I knew that voice. Jamie. Was the guy stalking me now?

I refused to turn around and look at him, though I knew I'd be faced with just that scenario soon enough since the only empty chairs were at the other end of the 'L' of the bar. I was about to be sitting exactly diagonal from his group.

I tried my best to maintain eye contact with Brad as he continued on with his story, but I swear I felt Jamie's gaze on me. It was like a living, breathing creature sliding over my skin in a soft caress. I managed to last a couple of minutes before I diverted my eyes, and then only for just a second. It was such a small quantity of time, but it was enough to see that he was looking devastatingly handsome. Of course he was. He was out to torture me.

Jamie was dressed casually in a light blue T-shirt that stretched across his upper body. I had a hard time not visualizing what he looked like out of that shirt, now that I'd seen for myself at the pool party what lay underneath. He looked like he'd recently showered, his hair darker than normal and a little more slicked back, though the long ends still curled up in the most frustrating way. Frustrating only because they begged for a girl to run her fingers through them, and I'd be doing no such thing.

When his gaze met mine, the corner of one of his lips curled up. He raised his beer in a small wave and the other two guys he was with turned to see who he was looking at. I knew Ben fairly well, but I wasn't sure who the other guy was. Regardless, I waved back at them in what I hoped was a casual way and returned my attention to Brad.

"You know those guys?" he asked, his interest clearly piqued.

"Yeah, through work." I didn't elaborate further. What could I say? The one with 'fuck me' eyes had actually gotten me off not long ago and I'd been trying unsuccessfully to get him out of my head since? Not likely.

"So what is it exactly that you do at work?" Brad asked.

I delved into describing my job as a nine-one-one operator, doing my best to ignore the fact that I could see Jamie from the corner of my eye. His voice would drift over from time-to-time, making it impossible to pretend he didn't exist.

"Would you excuse me for a moment?" I said distractedly. "I'm going to visit the restroom."

"Of course," Brad said politely.

I smiled at him and reached for my purse. As I made my way to the back of the bar, I walked right past the backs of Jamie, Ben, and the other guy. They all seemed to be engrossed in the game on the TV behind the bar anyway, shouting expletives at someone behind the glass screen.

When I reached the washroom, I set my purse on the counter, leaned on both hands, and stared at myself in the mirror. I didn't even need to use the facilities—I just needed a break from being under Jamie's watchful eye. I really needed to get my shit together where he was concerned. I needed to leave behind the memory of what had happened between us before it drove me mad. I'd thought I was making progress, but seeing him made it abundantly clear that was not the case.

He was just a guy, like any other guy, so why did he affect me so much?

Drawing a in deep breath, I closed my eyes. Alright. I was going to go out there and pay him no mind. He didn't have any control over me. No one did. I prided myself on being my own person and doing what I wanted, when I wanted. Jamie-freaking-McTavish was not going to change that.

Feeling slightly more composed, I fussed with my hair for a second, pulled my purse strap over my one shoulder so it crossed over my chest, then left. I was one step into the hall when someone grabbed my wrist and tugged me toward the back of the building.

"What the hell?" I whipped my head over to see Jamie pulling me toward the back door. When he turned so I was able to see his face, I almost wished he hadn't. His brows were drawn and his lips were pursed into a thin line. He didn't look happy.

I glanced down to see that he was wearing a perfectly faded pair of jeans with flip flops. Damn, his butt looked good in those jeans. *Ugh!* What was I thinking? He was acting like a Neanderthal dragging me out of here.

Pushing open the rear door with one hand, he pulled me out into the warm night air, the metal door making a loud thud behind us. He dropped my hand and spun to face me.

"What do think you're doing?" I asked incredulously, crossing my arms over my chest.

"Me? What're you doing, Jackie?" Somehow he was able to draw his brows even further over his eyes. It made him look almost scary.

"I *was* out on a date until you dragged me back here like the caveman that you are!"

His eyes flashed. "Is that guy the reason you won't go out with me?"

"What?" The quick change in topic left me trying to keep up.

"You heard me." He took a step closer, and my reaction was somewhat schizophrenic—my body wanted to be closer and, at the same time, my head was screaming at me to back away. I would not cower to him, though, I'd hold my ground.

I stood exactly where I was and brought my hands to my hips. "I won't go out with you because I don't want to. I don't even know you."

"Are you dating that guy?" he ground out.

"Duh. We're on a date," I said with attitude.

The back of his jaw began twitching. Damn it. Why did I feel the need to rile him up?

"Anyone can see you two aren't right for each other." He motioned to the building behind us. "There's zero chemistry."

I placed my hand at my waist and cocked a hip. Who the hell did he think he was, telling me what was right for me? "For your information, this is our first date. And *I'll* be the one to decide whether or not we're right for each other."

"Come on, Jackie." He sighed loudly. "You think that beaker in there can do for you what I can?"

He forced me back into the building behind me, then placed his leg between mine, pushing up so that his hard thigh pressed exactly where I wanted it to. But I'd never admit that to him. His own arousal was evident against my hip, and I stifled a moan and closed my eyes.

"Would you let him touch you the way you let me in that wine cellar? Does he get you hot and bothered the way I do?" He pushed up with his thigh again. "Does he?"

I opened my eyes, knowing they were pleading with him to just leave me alone. To accept what I was saying and move on. "I need to get back to my date," I whispered weakly, close to giving up the fight. It was near impossible for me to say no to this man.

He stared at me for a full minute, his gray eyes intense. A car horn honked somewhere far off and the sound of people wandering along the sidewalk filled the silence. "Fine. But you're not leaving until I give you a reminder of why we'd be so good together."

Before I could comprehend what he meant by that, he leaned in and fused his lips to mine. As if my hands had a mind of their own, they dove into Jamie's hair. But my legs were the worst offender. Without thinking, I wrapped them around his waist, and he pressed me against the brick wall with his body, his hands gripping my ass.

Our tongues met with intense fury, only serving to stoke the already raging fire between us. He knew exactly how to drive me wild, give me everything he had, overwhelm me and make me needy, only to pull back enough to leave me desperate for him. I was certain he'd be the same in the bedroom—intense and somehow controlled.

He cranked his hips up into my core, putting pressure on the place I needed it most. I moaned and, with no warning, his hands came around his back and unwrapped my legs from around his waist. I slid to the pavement on shaky legs as Jamie stepped back from me with a shit-eating grin on his face.

"See if pretty boy in there can get that reaction from you."

My mouth dropped open, gaping while I attempted to get my brain synapses firing again so I could come up with a witty retort. I had nothing.

Jamie stepped to the side and reached for the handle of the back door, swinging it wide open and gesturing for me to go back in. "Ladies first."

I wanted to stomp my feet like a petulant child at how I'd so easily played into his charms and allowed him to prove his point. Instead, I managed to gather myself enough that I walked by him, chin held high, like I had even a shred of dignity left. I continued down the hall into the main bar area and didn't turn to see if he'd followed. I didn't have to. I could feel his eyes raking up and down my body, and I knew he was close behind me.

I gave as natural a smile to Brad as I could give under the circumstances and rejoined him at the bar, setting my purse down.

"I was about to send out a search party," he laughed.

I forced a small chuckle, although I was completely preoccupied with the man who sat across the bar, the one I knew was watching my every move. I wouldn't give him the satisfaction of looking his way. I'd already managed to do enough to feed his ego this evening.

"You look a little flushed. You okay?" Brad asked with evident concern.

"Now that you mention it I'm not feeling that great." I rubbed my temples to help with my charade. "Mind if we cut the evening short? I think I need to go home and lay down." With my vibrator, I added only to myself.

"Of course, of course." Brad pushed his stool out and then came around to pull out my own. It was kind of sweet—I'd never had anyone try to pull out a bar chair for me before.

"I'm really sorry to have to take off like this," I said, grabbing my purse from the table and getting out of the chair to face him.

"No need to apologize. Maybe we can finish our date another time." He looked so hopeful I couldn't help feeling guilty for going out with him in the first place, knowing there was little chance it was going anywhere.

"Yeah, maybe." I gave him a small smile, then leaned in to give him a friendly hug.

"I'll walk you to your car."

"Not necessary, but thank you." I gave him a warm smile to ward off the guilt.

He shook his head. "I insist."

Relenting, I nodded and headed out with Brad in tow. I didn't seem destined to win any argument with the opposite sex tonight. Might as well quit while I was ahead.

# *Chapter Nine*

## JAMIE

How the hell had I let myself get roped into this?

I adjusted the belt on my uniform and ran a nervous hand through my hair. The hooting and hollering, coupled with interspersed giggles, could be heard from the makeshift backstage they'd erected in the country club's ballroom.

Three more bachelors to go, and I was due up for auction. Being that I was fairly new in town, I didn't think I could decline the invitation to participate in the charity bachelor auction. Don had asked me a couple months back, and I hadn't thought much of it. Now I wished I had declined.

I had more self-confidence than necessary on any given day, but somehow today I felt like I was being led to slaughter. What if no one bid on me? How fucking embarrassing would that be?

I heard the presenter call out the number ahead of mine, and the women scream in appreciation as the Ranger from Acadia National Park made his way out to the stage.

*Get your shit together, man.*

I shook my hands out and shifted my weight back and forth. There were more guys hanging around backstage waiting to be called. One had on a doctor's coat, while another looked like he belonged on a boat so I was guessing he was a fisherman. They milled around making conversation while I stood alone, seeming to be the only nervous one.

The volunteer funneling men onto the stage waved me over and, when they called my number, she practically pushed me out through the curtain. "Good luck," she called after me.

"Ladies, please welcome the newest member to our police force to the stage...Mr. Jamie McTavish." The crowd erupted into applause and cat calls as I sauntered over to the MC. Seems I'd been worried for nothing. A guy could get used to this. I smiled and pushed my chest out and my shoulders back. "Jamie enjoys keeping active on his days off, doing just about anything that'll keep his heart rate up. While his motto is that he'll try anything once, he draws the line at caviar. Jamie, why don't you say hi to the ladies." The aging man moved the mic in front of my face.

"Hey, ladies," I said in my lowest, sexiest voice.

They cheered again and some whistles could be heard, though I wasn't sure which direction they came from. I smiled wide again, confidence replacing my earlier nerves.

"Why don't we start the bidding at one hundred dollars...do I hear one hundred dollars?"

"One hundred dollars," someone yelled out from the crowd. I turned to my left, but I wasn't able to see who it was through all the people.

"Two hundred," a woman on the right side of the stage shouted. If my mother had still been alive, I was sure this woman would have closely resembled her. Her gray hair was short, permed, and she looked up at the stage from underneath a pair of thick glasses. Her pants were too high on her waist, and she was wearing those beige orthotic shoes a lot of the senior citizens seemed to wear.

It wasn't until I saw her that I'd given any thought as to who I might end up with tonight.

"Three hundred!"

This time when I turned to my other side, I realized the bidder had made her way to the front of the crowd. I smiled warmly at her. If I got stuck with her, it wouldn't be half bad. This woman looked to be in her early twenties with blond hair, blue eyes, and a slender body. However, there had been only one woman on my mind these past few weeks, and unfortunately it wasn't her.

"Four hundred!" the elderly lady called out. The woman wanted what she wanted, I thought with an inward chuckle.

The blonde's eyes darted over to her, and she smirked, appearing almost...predatory. "Six hundred," she said in a strong, confident voice.

Holy shit, someone just bid six hundred bucks on me.

"Wowee, can you believe it everyone? We're up to six hundred dollars already. Keep it coming! And don't forget that it's all going to a great cause. Who wouldn't want to spend an evening with all this?" The MC held his hand out and motioned from my head to my feet and back up like I was a prize on *The Price Is Right*.

All the attention of the crowd turned back to the older lady, who was biting nervously on the end of her finger. Finally, after a moment, she called out, "Seven hundred!"

The blonde rolled her eyes. "Eight hundred." She crossed her arms over her chest and pinned the elderly lady with a challenging gaze.

A woman standing beside the older lady shoved her with an elbow. The older lady chewed on her lip for a moment, looking unsure. Waving a hand in front of her, she said, "You can have him. I probably wouldn't know what to do with him anyway."

The crowd laughed, and the MC brought the mic to his mouth. "Eight hundred dollars going once...going twice..."

I glanced over to the blonde, who had a triumphant look on her face.

"And—"

"One thousand dollars!"

At the new bid, the entire room hushed, and the blonde woman's eyes bugged out of her head. She turned, searching the low murmuring throng for the person who had outbid her. My heart was fucking pounding in my chest, and I didn't have to wait to see her walk up through the parted crowd to know who it was—I'd recognize her voice anywhere.

My lips spread into a satisfied smile, and my dick twitched in my pants before I even set eyes on Jackie. Seems she was finally ready to acknowledge what I'd been telling her all along.

# *Chapter Ten*

## *Jackie*

I wasn't sure what had come over me, but when Chloe had told me that the woman bidding on Jamie was the girl her ex had cheated with, it was fair to say I was equal parts pissed and green with envy, yelling out my bid before I'd had a chance to really consider it.

I'd already been trying hard to control the jealousy surging through my veins at the thought of him going out with another woman. I wasn't able to control my mind from wondering if he'd do to her the same things he'd done to me. It was like a movie running through my head...a horror film, actually.

Seeing Jamie's smug grin as he looked over at me, and the way he puffed his chest out almost had me wishing I'd left him to her.

"We have a last minute bidder, folks! One thousand dollars! Seems there are a few women interested in seeing what tricks the new guy has up his sleeve. Let's hear it, ladies! Anyone want to enjoy an evening out with this fine gentleman for eleven hundred dollars?"

The MC couldn't be serious. Surely no one would

bid more than that.

As soon as the thought popped into my brain, the blonde bitch called out, "Eleven hundred!"

"Twelve hundred!" I shot back, surprising myself and everyone in the room.

"Thirteen hundred." She locked a lethal stare on me.

Two could play at this game. "Fourteen hundred." It was just the two us now, staring each other down in a death match to see who would back down first.

If possible, her eyes narrowed even more. "Fifteen hundred."

"Sixteen hundred," I said back without batting an eye. Obviously she had no idea just how competitive and stubborn I could be.

A few gasps came from the crowd. I'd been going to this fundraiser for years, and I was pretty sure no one had ever bid this high before. I didn't like it, but it was a charity that was near and dear to my heart so I took some solace in the fact that the money would be going to a good cause—even if I'd be eating Raman noodles for the next month.

She didn't say anything for a moment, and I knew I had her when she pressed her lips together.

The MC shouted, "Sixteen hundred going once...twice...*sold* to this fine young lady in the green dress."

"Oh, my God. I can't believe you bid that high," Chloe said, tugging on my arm with one hand, the other on her chest.

I turned to face my best friend. Her eyes were wide in surprise, but the pain of the reminder of what her ex had done to her, and with whom, was all over her face, and I didn't regret for a minute how much money I'd spent.

I patted her hand with mine, giving her a reassuring look. "I wasn't about to let that bitch get her claws in him."

Chloe leaned in and gave me a quick hug.

I hugged her back, then tugged her behind me. "Come on. I've gotta go pay for my bid, then let's get out of here."

We pushed our way to the back of the crowd as the MC brought the next bachelor out. I handed my credit card info over, perturbed with myself that I no doubt had fed Jamie's inflated ego, but, at the same time happy the money would be put to good use. Still, I wanted to get out of here before I was forced into a confrontation with him. When I told Chloe as much, her gaze darted behind me and a sly smile crossed her face. I had a good idea who was coming up behind me. I inwardly cringed.

"I've gotten mixed signals from women before, but you've got to be a world record holder by now," Jamie chuckled from behind me, coming to stand between me and Chloe.

With a half-hearted gesture, I motioned to him, and then to her. "Chloe, this is Jamie. Jamie, Chloe."

Jamie stuck his hand out to shake Chloe's. "Good to meet you."

"Same here," Chloe said, grinning. "I've heard a lot about you."

"Is that so?" Jamie arched a brow, amused. "Your friend here would lead me to believe she never thought of me at all." He glanced over at me, his expression challenging me to deny it.

Chloe's dark brown eyes darted to me and then back to Jamie. "Don't listen to her. She's just obsessed with keeping things uncomplicated."

"Hello..." I waved my hands in front of me. "Standing right here."

Jamie turned to face me, pinning an intense gaze on me with those steel-colored eyes. "Uncomplicated, huh?"

I raised my chin, feeling defiant. "I happen to like uncomplicated."

Chloe cleared her throat. "I'm going to leave you two to talk. I'll be outside when you're ready to leave, Jackie."

I nodded, but neither Jamie nor I removed our gaze from the other.

"So what was all that about?" Jamie crossed his hands over his chest and motioned behind him with his head.

"I wanted to donate to the cause." I shrugged, feigning nonchalance, unwilling to let him know how riled up I'd been at the thought of the other woman winning him.

He shook his head. "Not buying it. There's more to it than that."

I clenched my fists at my side. "Think what you want." I said, irritation ringing in my voice.

Jamie's gaze ran up and down the length of me and appeared a little glazed over by the time he'd reached my eyes again. "You look really beautiful tonight. The color of your dress brings out the green in your eyes."

Heat pooled between my thighs from the combination of his words and the way he looked at me with unadulterated lust. "Don't do that," I snapped.

"Do what?" His forehead creased.

"Turn a normal conversation into something sexual." I wasn't even sure why I was picking a fight with him. He wasn't the problem. I was irritated with myself, and at the utter lack of control I seemed to have when he was near.

"I was only saying you look nice tonight, not telling you I wanted to feel your lips wrapped around my cock— relax." He arched a brow, clearly amused with himself. God, he could be such an ass.

He must've been able to tell that the mental image of what he'd suggested had flashed through my head because a slow smirk spread across his face.

"There you go again." I let out a frustrated sigh. "And stop looking at me like that."

Now he seemed amused. "And how is that exactly?"

"Like I'm dessert."

He leaned in to speak directly into my ear. I tried to hold my breath so I wouldn't be forced to inhale his natural scent, the one I'd longed to smell again since I'd kissed him behind the bar. "Oh, but you will be dessert at the end of our date. I can't wait to taste you."

I inhaled a sharp breath and momentarily pressed my thighs together. Once I'd regained my composure I shoved into his chest, forcing him back and ignoring how hard his chest muscles were underneath my palms. "You're impossible."

He shrugged, not at all fazed by my frustration. "Maybe, but you like it."

God help me, but a part of me did. "I've got to get going. Chloe is waiting."

"Alright then. Enjoy the rest of your evening, Jackie. I know I will—imagining all the things we'll be doing on our date," he said with a cocky grin.

I narrowed my eyes. "Don't count on it."

He laughed, his eyes full of mirth. "Oh, Jackie. Haven't you figured it out yet? We're a foregone conclusion."

The truth of his words slammed into me like a Mac truck, and I stumbled back a step, then pivoted on my heel and booked it out of there as fast as my stilettos would allow. No way was I tempting fate and giving myself to a man like Jamie—one that had 'Caution: Police Line Do Not Cross' tape all over it.

# Chapter Eleven

## JAMIE

I couldn't afford to fuck this up. I was more than certain this was my only shot to convince Jackie to start seeing me. If tonight didn't go well, that would be it. She wouldn't be giving me another chance. For whatever reason, I'd lucked into our date tonight, and I was going to make good use of it.

I climbed the steps to her house, more anxious than I could remember being in a long time. She'd attempted to give me some bullshit excuse about meeting me at the restaurant rather than having me pick her up. I'd let her know it wasn't an option. I had, after all, seen her ditch her last date at the bar and I refused to be relegated to the same treatment as that poindexter had gotten. Besides, we weren't going to a restaurant. I had other plans for us. Plans I was hoping she'd like.

I knocked on the door, and Jackie swung it open, looking even more gorgeous than she usually did. How was that even possible? She was wearing a light blouse that tied just below her belly button. I had no idea what it was made of, but it was flowy with a V-neck that showed just enough of her cleavage to keep it on your mind all night. Beige dress shorts and strappy gold heels accented her toned legs. Jackie had nice legs. Hell, Jackie had nice everything.

"You look exceptional," I said, still gawking.

She drew in a deep breath. "Thank you." She glanced down to the flowers I held in my hand, knocking me out of my trance.

I cleared my throat. "These are for you." I held them out for her, and she smiled, bringing the cluster forward to sniff them. When her forehead wrinkled in confusion, I knew she'd spotted the note I'd placed in the middle.

She pulled them away from her face and reached for the piece of paper. "What's this?"

"Take a look." I nodded toward it.

She stepped back into her entryway and motioned for me to follow before she turned and set the flowers down on a table and pulled the paper out of its envelope. As a sort of joke, and a way to break the ice, I'd purchased a Triple A membership for her. I hated the idea of her being stranded again with no one to help her.

She laughed. "Thank you for this." She held the paper up in her hand. "Hopefully I won't need to use it too often." There was a twinkle in her green eyes, and I think it was the first time she'd ever actually looked at me that way. I'd seen lust and need, irritation and frustration, but never thankfulness or appreciation.

I cleared my throat. "I'd like to start over...on this date tonight. I want to wipe the slate clean and start fresh."

She twisted her lips for a minute, then nodded. "Okay then." Picking up the flowers off her entry table, she said, "Let me just put these in some water before we go."

As she retreated toward the back of the house, I took in my surroundings, curious about the place she called home. It was a cute little bungalow, though the art on the walls was a little bright for my liking. A fireplace sat in the center of the living room, photographs placed strategically on the mantle. There was one of her and the girl I had met at the auction, another of what I guessed was her and her mother, and the largest frame belonged to a portrait of a man in a police dress uniform. The photograph was obviously older based on the coloring. Was that her dad?

"Ready to roll?" Jackie asked as she made her way back up the hall.

"Yep. Nice place you have here," I complimented.

"Thanks. I haven't decided whether I'm going to stay here or look for something else to rent when my lease is up in a few months."

*Huh.* "Oh, I assumed you owned it." She had a good job. There was no reason why she'd have to rent.

"No, I like to move around, switch it up, leave my options open." She shrugged. "I'm not one to get too attached to where I'm staying."

I found it telling that she'd referred to it as the place she was staying, not living, but I kept that to myself. She appeared to be relaxed in my presence tonight, and I didn't want anything to fuck that up. I gave her a relaxed smile. "Well, it's a nice spot anyway."

She smiled back and grabbed her purse from the table. "Shall we?"

Once we were settled in my truck and pulling away from her house, she turned to face me. "So, where are we going?"

Things were going well so far—Jackie's attitude toward me was better than I'd ever seen it. I hoped that what came out of my mouth next wouldn't ruin that. "I thought we could go to my place for dinner. I ordered some food from one of the restaurants on Main Street. We have to swing by there and pick it up." I shrugged. "I just thought it would be nicer than being in a crowded, noisy restaurant on a Saturday night at the height of tourist season."

"Jamie..." she said, sounding unsure.

"Listen, I didn't plan it as some way of trying to get in your pants." I placed my hand on her shoulder and looked her straight in the eye. "Honestly. I want to get to know you better, that's all. If you're more comfortable staying at the restaurant to eat, we can do that."

Jackie fidgeted in her seat, seeming unsure. "No, no it's fine. As long as you promise to drive me home whenever I want."

"Of course. I'll be a complete gentleman." I smiled wide, feeling victorious.

She smirked. "I'll believe that when I see it."

I shook my head and chuckled softly. "Oh, ye of little faith."

I meant it, though. Tonight was about getting to know the paradox of a woman that was sitting beside me and ensuring she wanted to spend more time with me in the future.

We arrived at my place a half hour later. When I'd moved to Bar Harbor, I'd bought a place a little outside of town, surrounded by woods. It wasn't huge, but it was a comfortable size, and I'd been slowly picking away at home renovation projects to make it even more welcoming.

It was a raised bungalow with a wraparound porch that I enjoyed relaxing on with a beer. At the moment, I was enjoying trailing behind Jackie on the stairs because it gave me another fine view of her assets.

We reached the top of the stairs, and I led her across the deck to the door. Using the hand that wasn't holding the bag of food, I reached in my pocket for the key and unlocked the door, then stepped to the side. "Ladies first."

"You're giving me too much credit." She laughed and walked past me into the house. The slight citrus scent I was beginning to attribute to her wafted past me.

"This is a really nice place." She spun around to face me with a warm smile. "Nothing at all like the bachelor pad I've been picturing."

I chuckled, moving past her and through the living room into the open concept kitchen. "I'm a little too old for anything like that now."

"How old are you?" she asked, coming to stand on the opposite side of the center island and leaning forward on her hands. Her emerald eyes were alight with mischief.

"Almost thirty," I said openly as I pulled the food out of the bags. Turning, I grabbed a couple plates from the cupboard behind me.

"You're practically an old man." She grinned and arched a brow.

"Easy there. I'm pretty sure you're not that far off." I winked playfully at her.

"Can I help?" Jackie offered as I began removing the lids.

"No, no. You paid good money for this date. You just relax."

She appeared momentarily embarrassed, then laughed a little. "For the amount of money I paid for this date you'd better be serving lobster and steak."

"Such high maintenance." I tsked, shaking my head in an amused way. "You're close. I opted for the lobster, but not the steak," I said as I portioned out both of our dinners onto the plates. "Can I get you something to drink? I picked up a good bottle of wine earlier today."

"Wine sounds great."

I walked over to the glass-fronted cupboard that

held the four wine glasses I owned and grabbed a pair. As I pulled the white wine from the fridge, I reflected on how normal this felt, how comfortable...like we were a real couple. And most surprising—how much I enjoyed the feeling. I'd dated a couple of girls seriously, but the last one had been years prior. I wasn't used to this sort-of thing, and if I'm honest I hadn't missed it at all. I was beginning to see what the appeal was.

"Where would you like to eat?" I asked her glancing around my place. "We can sit at the kitchen table or at the breakfast bar..."

Jackie surveyed the surroundings. "Would it be weird if we sat on the floor around the coffee table in the living room?"

I shook my head. "Not at all."

"Your deck is lovely, but I don't want to be swatting away all the critters looking for a free meal."

"Good point." I smiled at her. "Why don't you grab the silverware off the counter and I'll handle the plates."

A few minutes later, we were settled in—our plates in front of us, along with our wine. I'd turned on some music to help set the mood and, even though it was summer, I turned the fire on for ambiance. I found myself wanting Jackie to be comfortable in my house. I wanted her to *want* to return.

We each took a few bites of our meal, not saying anything. Jackie picked up her wine glass and took a sip. "Your fireplace is lovely."

"Thanks. I just finished it a couple weeks ago. I'm no expert, but I've been taking on some home renovation projects since I moved in." My response had been casual, but the truth was that hoisting the reclaimed wood mantle up and setting it overtop of the stone fireplace had been one hell of a job.

Jackie speared some pasta with her fork and

wrapped her lips around the twines. "Mmm, this is good." She held her hand in front of her mouth while she chewed and, when she'd swallowed, asked, "So if you're from Boston, why don't I hear an accent?"

I chuckled. "I'm not from there originally."

"What brought you to Maine then?"

I set my fork down beside my plate, finding the answer to her question did little to inspire my appetite. My discomfort must've shown on my face.

"I'm sorry did I say something wrong?" She reached forward and put her hand on top of mine. The physical contact with her was comforting.

I shook my head. "No, not at all. It's just not a lot of fun to talk about. My dad lives here. He became ill so I moved here to keep an eye on him." I shrugged and worked to suppress my emotions, not wanting to delve into too heavy of topics tonight.

Jackie's expression looked forlorn. "I'm sorry. I'm assuming your mom isn't around?"

"No," I frowned. "She passed away some years ago."

"Geez, I'm just hitting on every happy subject tonight aren't I?"

I turned my hand over so that I could grasp hers, accepting her comfort. "It was a while ago, and I've come to terms with it." I still missed my mom, but watching her suffer any longer, trying to fight a disease she wasn't winning the battle with, would have been worse.

"Still, you must miss her." Jackie swallowed hard.

"You talk like you know what that feels like," I said carefully, hoping she'd open up to me. There had been something in the tone of her voice that sounded like she was speaking from experience.

She shrugged, trying to play it off. "Maybe. Anyway, what's wrong with your dad?"

I let her get away with changing the topic because

she obviously didn't want to discuss it, and I had no intention of pushing her this soon and scaring her off.

"He has early onset Alzheimer's." My stomach clenched just saying the words. "Most days he's okay. Days that he has an episode are difficult."

Jackie squeezed my hand. "I'm so sorry." Her sympathy and support eased my discomfort. Since I was newer in town there wasn't really anyone in my life for me to talk about my dad's situation with.

"It is what it is. Best I can do is help where I can."

Jackie pursed her lips for a moment, looking reflective. "How are you adjusting to small town Bar Harbor? That's quite a change from Boston, I imagine."

"It is. In some ways I've enjoyed it, though." I very obviously drew my gaze up and down her body. She laughed good-naturedly. Being serious again I said, "No sense pining away about what can't be."

Jackie set her fork down beside her plate and rested her chin on her hand. "I like that philosophy. It's so true."

We spent the rest of dinner talking and getting to know each other better. I found out that she loved dogs, but didn't want the responsibility or commitment of having one, that she briefly considered opening a tourist shop on Main Street before she decided to pursue becoming a nine-one-one operator, and that the part that irked her the most when we first met was me calling her ma'am. I had a good laugh over that one.

When we'd finished eating, we were both curled up on opposite ends of the couch, a wine glass in hand. Perhaps it was the wine that had loosened my tongue, but I couldn't resist asking about the picture on the mantle of her fireplace.

"I noticed the picture on your mantle of the cop..." I trailed off, hoping she'd see where I was going and fill in the blanks.

Jackie shifted in her seat and cleared her throat. "It's my father."

It was what I'd suspected, but it still surprised me a bit. "Is he on the force locally?" Maybe I'd run into her father and had no idea.

She gave her head a small shake. "No. My dad is deceased."

Fuck. Way to go, nimrod. Real smooth. "I'm so sorry," I said, cringing.

"It was a long time ago," she whispered. "Like you said...you get used to it." She took a steadying breath and blinked back tears.

I wouldn't press. Obviously whatever had happened still upset her, and I wanted her to remember this night in a positive light. I was determined not to mess this up.

ELISABETH GRACE

# Chapter Twelve

## Jackie

"Would you like to dance?" Jamie held his hand out to me.

"What?" I glanced around the living room. "Here?" The gesture brought a warm feeling to my chest. One that had already been growing before he'd brought up the subject of my dad. I was determined not to let what had happened sixteen years ago affect what had, so far, been a wonderful evening.

"Yes, here." He smiled and I swear it brought out the green that I sometimes saw in his gray eyes.

"Sure." I was usually up for almost anything—why not this? I leaned forward to set my wine glass on the coffee table as he'd done a moment earlier, and I then took his hand. Tingles ran up my arm from our point of contact, and I didn't think I was alone in my reaction. His gaze darted up to mine and held steady as we both rose from the couch.

We made our way to the front of the fireplace as Hallelujah by K.D. Lang began playing and her soothing voice filled the room. Jamie wrapped me in his arms, pulling me close. I leaned my head on his chest, inhaling his masculine scent and enjoying the feeling of being surrounded by him.

*I could get used to this.* It was a fleeting thought, but it scared me nonetheless.

As we swayed back and forth, I realized the feeling was safety and security. In some ways I hadn't felt that since before I'd lost my dad. Ever since his death, I'd been afraid to love anything too much, lest it be taken away. My mom and Chloe had been the only exceptions, and that was only because they were in my heart long before my father was murdered.

I squeezed Jamie a little at that revelation. I didn't know what I was going to do with it, but there it was. He pulled back and looked down at me, brushing his knuckles along my cheek.

"Hey, is everything okay?" His gray eyes were filled with concern.

"Everything is great," I said with far too much emotion.

"You sure? You look...I don't know. Like you have something heavy on your mind."

I blew out a breath. God, could this man read me. "I'm sure." I lowered my head back down onto his chest, content to hear the strong sound of his heart beating beneath it. The song changed to one that I'd long loved and thought was sexy.

We swayed to the melody, brushing our bodies up against one another. I loved the feel of Jamie's back muscles rippling underneath my hands as he moved. Without warning, he stopped, his eyes searching my face. For what, I don't know.

"I really like you, Jackie. A lot." Evidence of his arousal grew against my stomach, leaving a tingling feeling at the juncture of my thighs. It was exhilarating knowing that I affected him that way. My nipples beaded, and he must've felt it because his hand pressed me tighter to him.

Fire was dancing in my veins. I didn't want to talk about feelings right now. My body wanted this man—craved him like I'd never craved another. Without hesitation, I reached up on my tippy toes and brought my mouth to his.

He gave in immediately, no fight, and pressed me closer, while his tongue ran along the seam of my mouth. I parted my lips and threaded my hands into his hair, working my fingers through the golden strands and loving the silky feel of the curled ends.

Jamie's hand trailed a path down my back until he cupped my ass, giving it a squeeze. A small whimper escaped me, which would've been embarrassing if I hadn't been so turned on.

I'm not sure how long we stood in front of the fire making out. It felt like forever as we learned one another's mouths and set our own pace and rhythm that seemed to drive each of us wild.

"I want you so badly," Jamie murmured against my lips. He dipped his head and kissed along my neck, using his tongue to trace the shell of my ear.

I shivered in response and leaned my head back, wanting more. "I want you, too," I breathed out.

"Are you ready to admit we'd be good together?" His lips were back on mine now, preventing me from answering, which suited me fine. I wouldn't have known what to say anyway.

"Where is your bedroom?" I asked breathlessly, pulling away from his kiss.

His eyes were hooded, the green in them more predominant than normal. "I don't want you thinking this is why I invited you here tonight," he said in a serious tone.

"If a woman asks where your bedroom is, you tell her," I said, just as seriously.

A half-smile tugged at the corner of his lips. "Follow me."

He grabbed my hand and practically dragged me down the hall that ran off of the kitchen until we arrived at a door at the end. Reaching for the handle, he glanced at me over his shoulder. "If we go in here...I'm not letting you out until I've had you. Is that something you're prepared for?" His gaze was full of stark, demanding need.

My breath hitched. God, I loved when he talked like that. I never had to imagine what he wanted or how he was feeling.

I nodded my head slowly. I was ready. We'd been practically dancing around this dalliance since our first meeting.

Jamie gave one quick jerk of his head and opened the door.

The room itself wasn't what I expected, not that I had expected anything. No, I hadn't been daydreaming about being in this exact position at all since the wine cellar.

It was tastefully decorated in shades of brown and green, with a coordinating bedspread. I was sure, if the guys down at the station had seen it, he'd be mocked endlessly. And if Jamie himself didn't exude pure rugged maleness, it might've come off as metrosexual, it was so well coordinated.

The king-sized bed was centered in the middle of the room with a wrought iron headboard displaying an intricate pattern, and a dark wood nightstand that matched the dresser sat on the right side of the bed.

Jamie turned to face me with a heated gaze and awareness crackled between us. "I want to undress you. Slowly. I've been imagining this since I first laid eyes on you, and I intend to take my time and enjoy it."

My breathing became shallow as he unbuttoned my shirt one button at a time, beginning with the bottom one and working his way up. His fingers brushed my heated skin as he dipped underneath to loosen each button. I closed my eyes, savoring the sensation. When he reached the top, he used both hands to slide my shirt down my arms until gravity took over and sent the material fluttering to the wood floor.

Now I stood in front of him, wearing only a black lace bra on my upper half. His eyes took me in with no shame as he brought both hands up and squeezed them. I groaned low in my throat, my head falling back. He unclasped my bra and it fell to the floor, then suddenly, Jamie dropped to his knees in front of me. I sucked in a breath.

He slid his fingers underneath my waistband, popping the button on my shorts and then pulling down the zipper agonizingly slow. I was desperate for him to remove them—they now felt way too restrictive. Placing his hands on my hips, he pulled the fabric down until it was at my ankles. I lifted one leg, then the other to remove them completely. Jamie tossed them to the side and there was something so intrinsically male and virile about the action that wetness pooled between my thighs.

Jamie's fingers slid up the side of my matching lace thong, then, in one quick swoop, he pulled the delicate fabric to the side, giving him a full view of my most intimate place. "You're completely bare." His eyes darted up to mine, looking for an explanation since I hadn't been this way a couple weeks ago when he'd explored me at the party.

I couldn't help but blush at having to provide a reason. "I told the girl that does my waxing to try something different this time."

Jamie grinned wide. "I like it." He leaned in and tasted me, pressing his tongue between my folds. I whimpered again, my legs shaking ever so slightly.

"Get on the bed." He stood and took my hand again, leading me across the room.

I crawled along the bed until I lay on my back, gazing up at him standing at the edge. "I'm feeling a little like we aren't on equal footing here, what with me practically naked and you with all those clothes on." I grinned playfully, not at all self-conscious. I worked hard to maintain this body, but it wouldn't have mattered...I'd always figured that most men were happy with a naked woman in front of them, regardless of whether or not she had a perfect body.

He chuckled low in his throat and undid his pants, shedding them without much effort. Underneath, he was wearing black boxer briefs that hugged his assets nicely, and I was now certain I'd been right about him being well-endowed.

His heavy-lidded gaze pinned me to the mattress as he dipped his thumbs into either side of his boxers and pulled them down, kicking them to the side as his erection sprang free. His socks were next, then he crawled up beside me with a feral look in his eye, like a lion stalking its prey. I was more than happy to play the role of the victim in that moment.

When he reached my body, his tongue lined a trail from my ankle up over my knee, along my inner thigh, over the lace of my panties and further up, stopping at my breasts and biting down lightly on one of my nipples. I arched my back up in response. He sucked my other nipple into his mouth, swirling his tongue around the tightened tip.

I dug my hands into his hair, loving that it was long enough to really grip, while he played with my breasts, sucking and nipping until I was a moaning, panting mess underneath him.

"You can't even imagine all the times I've thought about doing this to you," Jamie said in a slow, hot whisper against my heated flesh as he trailed a path with his tongue toward my center. He sucked at me over top of the lace and the sensation was just enough to make me wild, but not quite enough to send me over the edge.

I pulled on Jamie's hair while simultaneously pushing his face into me, begging for more friction. He chuckled against me and put me out of my misery by pulling my drenched thong down my legs.

His large hands gripped the backside of my knees and spread me so I was bared to him. "Such a beautiful pussy," he said with a note of reverence.

Oh God, his words. I could almost come from his words. "Jamie," I breathed out. Asking for what exactly, I wasn't sure.

Pressing my legs apart further and making sure I couldn't move, he leaned in and licked me, focusing on my swollen bud—sucking, pulling, and teasing it until I thought I'd lose my mind. Heat raced through my veins, centering at the apex of my thighs and, before I knew it, my orgasm overtook me with the force of an atom bomb, pummeling my head and shoulders down into the mattress as I tried bucking up off the bed. Jamie held me down and continued his assault, bringing me down slowly until I finally came back to myself.

Holy fuck Batman.

For a long moment, I lay there sated until I slowly opened my eyes. I was surprised to see him on his knees, staring down at me with such intensity that the connection between us felt as if it were almost a tangible thing. Like if I looked hard enough I'd see the tendrils of attachment growing like vines from each of us, meeting in the middle and wrapping around each other.

We both stayed there, gazing at each other. For seconds or minutes, I didn't know, but it was long enough to know that I was in deep shit because whether I had wanted it to happen or not, I was feeling something for Jamie—something deep and real.

"You on the pill?" he asked. I nodded, biting my lip. "I'm clean. Anything I need to know?" I shook my head, unable to speak under the weight of his stare.

Still maintaining eye contact with me, he reached for my ankle, leaned in, and brought my leg up so it rested over his shoulder. I instinctively wrapped my other leg around his waist while he gripped the base of his cock and brought it to my entrance.

"That was only the beginning of what I have in store for you, sweetheart." He pushed in slow yet forcefully, allowing my body time to adjust, all while pinning me with the same intensity in his eyes.

He began leisurely at first, pulling out and pushing in, unhurried and almost lazily until he increased his pace—steadily building up a rhythm until he was pounding his hard length in and out of me. I whimpered and strained against him, my sounds ragged with need.

Our position had him so deep inside me that it wasn't long before I felt the stirrings of another orgasm. Jamie's one hand gripped my ankle that was resting near his head and, when he moved it down to palm my breast and pull hard on my nipple, a fierce orgasm ripped through me. I cried out and clenched around him and, with a few jerky thrusts, he followed behind me, yelling out my name the way only a satisfied man could.

My chest heaving, I let me my leg drop, and he came to rest on top of me, shifting himself so that all his weight wasn't on me. It took a minute for us both to catch our breath, our skin slick with sweat, until he finally moved off of me to spoon me from behind.

That was when the panic set in.

I'd allowed Jamie to hurtle past all my defenses—defenses I'd spent years perfecting, and yet he'd toppled the wall as easily as if it were made of straw.

My heart rate picked up with this realization and, despite what we'd done, adrenaline surged anew through my veins.

*I need to get out of here.*

I tried to shift myself away from Jamie so I could get off the bed and find my clothes, but his arm around my waist pulled me back into him.

"I should get going," I said, trying not to let my panic come through in my tone.

He didn't respond, and I waited a minute before trying to pull away again, but Jamie's iron grip was too strong.

"Jackie, are you pushing me away?" he asked with a slight tremor to his voice. "I'm not the only one that feels this between us, am I?" he whispered.

I swallowed past the lump in my throat. No, he wasn't the only one. I felt it, too. And it was becoming increasingly difficult to pretend I didn't. I just couldn't help feeling like I was at a crossroads.

Taking a deep breath, I sought the courage to be honest with him. When I confessed to him how royally messed up I was, I wouldn't have to worry about leaving, he'd be pushing me out of his bed.

"I'm afraid," I said simply.

"Afraid of what?" He brushed an errant hair away from my face as he shifted so he was on top of me. For some reason, the gesture made me feel cherished, loved.

"Afraid of losing you," I whispered. I looked over his shoulder, suddenly unable to maintain eye contact with how vulnerable I felt.

"But we've barely even begun," he said, surprised but tender. "How could you be scared of losing me?"

"Because you're a cop."

Jamie stared down, waiting for me to explain further.

I gave a sad sigh, unshed tears burning behind my eyes. "You saw the picture of my dad on my mantle...he was killed when I was ten. He answered a domestic violence call one day and, before he'd even knocked on the door, the guy blew a hole through the door with a shotgun." My voice tremored and I inhaled a deep breath to compose myself. "My dad bled out before help could arrive."

"Oh, Jackie." Jamie wrapped his arms around me, pulling me up off the mattress and holding me to him. He clutched me so tight and his despair for me was so palpable, I succumbed to my tears. I wept in his arms, reliving in my head the pain of that day. Of seeing a cruiser pull up in my driveway and running outside, thinking it was my dad stopping by like he sometimes did when he was on shift. But then I heard my mother's screams from the front porch behind me as Don stepped out of the car, not my father. My ten-year-old self knew something was terribly wrong, but not exactly what, and as I sobbed into Jaime's naked chest, I recalled that final moment—the moment before everything had changed, before I'd known with certainty that my father was dead.

Jamie held me tight while I continued to weep, his large hands rubbing my back. He didn't whisper words of comfort that wouldn't hit their mark, he didn't try to tell me it would all be okay. He just let me purge everything I'd held inside for so long. I was unsure why I was so comfortable around him and willing to divulge what to date, had been the most painful period of my life.

When I had no more tears to cry, and my eyes burned and my throat hurt, he pulled away just enough to wipe the final saltwater away with his thumbs. "I'm so, so sorry." He leaned in to kiss my forehead. "Nothing I can say will take away from the tragedy of what happened. But now I have a better understanding of why you have your reservations about dating a cop."

"I'm fucked up, I know." I sniffed and wiped underneath my nose, not worrying about how unattractive it was.

"No, no you're not. Don't say that."

I leaned back so my head rested on the pillow again, Jamie still on top of me.

"I've watched my mom mourn my dad for sixteen years now. Sixteen years." I squeezed my eyes shut. When I opened them, Jamie was looking down on me in confusion.

"What do you mean?"

"I've grieved my dad, of course. But my mom was never able to move on. She hasn't dated since his death, his picture is still everywhere in her house, some of his clothes are still hanging in their closet." I inhaled deeply, holding my breath for a moment, then I whispered, "I don't want to be like her someday."

Jamie sighed. "Nothing is going to happen to me."

He sounded so sure. I shook my head, almost frantically. "You don't know that."

Jamie cradled my face in his hands. "Maybe not, but you can't not live your life because you're afraid something *might* happen. If something is going to happen, it'll happen anyway. You might as well live life to the fullest and enjoy the ride—wherever it leads."

Looking into his eyes, so insistent, I almost believed he was right. Almost. But I couldn't let go entirely to the mantra I'd been carrying inside me for so long.

"I really should be going." I shifted away from him on the mattress. "Can you drive me home?"

He stared at me for a moment, silent and still. "We

should talk about this."

"I just want to go home right now," I whispered, a pleading edge to my voice. I'd already divulged more of myself than I'd normally be willing to and I couldn't handle anymore tonight.

His lips pursed, but he nodded. "Okay."

A half hour later, Jamie pulled his truck up my driveway. He'd been silent the entire drive home. I knew he was mentally running over what I'd told him, probably trying to think of some way to get me to see reason. I wasn't sure that was possible. I'd been this way almost as long as I could remember...held onto that mantra, grabbing hold of it like it was a life preserver and I was lost in the open sea.

"Thanks for driving me. Sorry it's so late." I didn't have the nerve to glance over at him. I wasn't sure what I would see and that scared me.

"Jackie, look at me," he said, his voice soft. Jamie's hand gripped my chin and forced me to turn in his direction. He looked intent, purposeful. "I had an amazing evening with you, and I want to do it again." He leaned forward and gave me a chaste kiss on the lips. "Please tell me we can do it again."

I gave him a small smile. "I've never been asked for a repeat in the sac quite like that. You need to work on your game," I teased, trying to lighten the mood.

Jamie didn't laugh, didn't even quirk a smile. "I'm not referring to us fucking again. That's bound to happen if we spend any amount of time together. We have too much chemistry for it not to." His gaze was penetrating, but softened some before he continued. "I want to spend more time with you. Outside of the bedroom."

I sucked my bottom lip into my mouth, unsure what to say. I really liked Jamie. My feelings for him were more intense than they'd been with anyone before him. But I didn't want to fall for him. I wasn't even sure I could let my guard down enough for that to happen, but still, I was afraid to find out.

"Please say yes," Jamie whispered. His voice was steady, but his eyes were pleading.

I wanted to say no. Correction. I wanted to *want* to say no. But damn it, I didn't have the strength. As much as the panic was bubbling up inside of me again, I couldn't. Not when he was looking at me like that. "Fine."

His eyebrows drew down. "Fine isn't exactly the enthusiastic response I was hoping for, but I'll take what I can get. Thank you." He leaned forward, pressing his lips to mine again and holding them there a moment. I breathed in his scent, finding it brought a small amount of ease after what I'd just agreed to. When he pulled away, there was hope in his eyes. "You go get some sleep. I'll call you this week, and we can figure out what night will work between both our shifts."

I nodded and stepped out of the truck, liking the feel of the cool summer night air on my face. I felt emotionally exhausted as I headed up my porch steps. I'd definitely be getting sleep tonight. Well, hopefully. As I unlocked the door and entered my home, I gave Jamie a small wave then shut the door. Tossing my purse on the front hall table, I walked to the kitchen in search of a glass of water.

The instant I saw the vase with the flowers Jamie had given me in the middle of my kitchen table, I burst into tears. God, why did I have to be so fucked up? Why couldn't I be like any other girl who would probably rejoice in the fact that a man like Jamie wanted them?

I sank down into the seat, my elbows on the table, the heels of my hands on my forehead, and I let the tears fall. It'd been years since I'd cried like this, and now I'd done it twice in one evening. It had been so long since I'd let someone get close enough to me that they had the ability to make me cry. That was the most frightening thought of all. Because whether I wanted him to or not didn't seem to matter. Jamie had already stolen a piece of my heart. And like a thief in the night, I hadn't even realized he'd done it until it was too late.

# Chapter Thirteen

## JAMIE

It took some planning with both of our crazy shifts, but we were able to meet up mid-week. We'd decided I would meet Jackie at Geddy's Bar after my shift was up. I'd showered and changed quickly at work to race over to meet her.

I'd thought of little but her since I'd dropped her at her place on the weekend. After she'd confided in me about why she didn't want to date a cop, everything clicked into place—why she continued to deny our connection, her hard and fast rule about not dating any emergency service personnel.

I didn't like what she'd had to tell me, but I understood. I couldn't imagine having my father ripped away from me at such a young age. My own father was being taken from me as an adult—slowly and in stages.

Walking into the restaurant, I spotted Jackie at a table in the center of the space. She gave me a wary smile as I approached, which I supposed was better than her running off. Or worse, standing me up. I knew this was new territory for her. I needed to keep that in mind.

"You look as stunning as ever." I leaned in and gave

her a innocent kiss on the mouth before taking my own seat. If I thought I could get away with more, I would have. I'd been desperate to taste her lips again since I'd last left her.

"Thank you." A faint blush crept over her cheeks, reminding me of how she had looked after she'd orgasmed. "How was your shift?"

I shrugged. "Nothing too exciting. Some teenage prank stuff and a dispute between neighbors over a barking dog." I rolled my eyes.

She laughed for a second before the waitress approached the table. We ordered a pair of beers and, by the time she had returned to the table, the conversation had moved on.

"So tell me...what is the craziest nine-one-one call you've ever gotten? I'm sure you must hear some interesting stuff. I know we do," I said.

She looked up to the ceiling for a second, elongating her neck, which was like an invitation to lean in and suck on it. Somehow I was able to keep my ass in my seat.

"Once, when I had only been there for a few months, this guy called in to report that his cable had gone out in the middle of *Breaking Bad*." She chuckled. "I'm laughing now, but it wasn't funny at the time."

"There should be some kind of penalty when people abuse the service," I said, disgusted.

"Tell me about it. He was drunk, needless to say. Probably high, too." She rolled her emerald eyes, and I found it completely endearing. "So what's your best story from the trenches?"

"That's an easy one. Back in Boston we got a call from a couple who were holed up in their apartment bathroom because their cat had gone crazy."

She scrunched up her forehead. "What does that mean, the cat went crazy?"

I leaned forward, grinning. "Picture letting a cherry bomb off in a box, rocketing around in there every which way. Only it's a cat with claws, panicked and stuck in a small apartment and once it latches on to you, it's next to impossible to get off."

Jackie laughed and it lit up her eyes. "Wow, now I know why I was never a cat person." She lifted her drink to her mouth and ran her tongue over her bottom lip when a small drop escaped. It was an innocent act, but it was distracting to my dirty mind.

I nodded. "It took two animal control personnel and four officers, two hours to  catch the cat before the people were able to come out of the bathroom. When they did, they had to go to the hospital to be treated so they wouldn't develop an infection from all the scratches. They were covered from head to toe."

Jackie brought her hand to her chest. "Oh, my God. That's awful."

"I wish I could've videotaped it. Watching all these tough macho guys scared of a small cat and trying to catch this thing without getting their eyes scratched out was hysterical." I started laughing just remembering it all. I was laughing so hard that I hadn't noticed some guy had approached our table.

"Hey, Jackie." He was a little younger than I was, and he ignored me as he leaned across the table, looking directly at her.

She shifted in her seat, her eyes darting between me and him. "Hey, Terry."

"I haven't heard from you lately. I was thinking about you the other day and then here you are." He gave her a cheesy, suave smile, and there was something in his tone that I didn't like...something that suggested they knew each other on more than just a friendly basis.

"Hey, I'm Jamie." I stuck my hand out across the

93

ELISABETH GRACE

table to shake his. "Good to meet you." The tone of my voice implied I wasn't actually happy to meet him, but that suited me fine.

He glanced briefly over his shoulder at me. "Hey, man." Ignoring my outstretched hand, he turned his attention back to Jackie.

Jackie's face was colored red now. "I'm kind of busy right now. Can we catch up another time?" The expression on her face was imploring him to go away.

"Sure, doll. I'll leave you to it." I clenched my fist under the table and drew in a breath to calm myself. "But be sure to give me a call soon." He backed away from the table and gave her a onceover, making it no mystery what was on his mind. "It's been too long." Then he sauntered away.

I suddenly felt like punching something. Or someone. Mainly him.

"Sorry about that." Jackie cringed.

I wasn't sure if I should ask what the hell that was all about or just leave it. I decided that some douchebag wasn't worth ruining this date over, so I'd ignore the prick for now. There was something I *was* curious about, though.

"I'm surprised that, with everything that happened with your dad, you chose to get into the profession you did."

She looked down to the table for a moment, taking a thoughtful sip of her beer. "In some ways, I think it's because of what happened." She pressed her plump lips together. "I could never be a cop like my dad, not after what happened. But helping people in need and doing your civic duty was so important to him. I can remember him talking about it to me when I was little. Being a nine-one-one Operator was a way to honor my dad and help out people in need at the same time, I guess."

I nodded my head slowly. "I get it."

Jackie shrugged. "It's probably the only healthy way I've dealt with losing him. Obviously I haven't mastered the matters of the heart yet." She gave a humorless chuckle.

"I'm doing my best to rectify that," I said, looking into her eyes with all the softness and sincerity I could muster.

"I know." She picked at the label on her beer for moment, then drew in a deep breath and gave me a sad smile. I was about to change the subject when her gaze flicked behind me, and her expression turned from melancholy to anger in the time it took her to blink.

"What's the matter?" I craned my neck to look behind me. She'd seemed to be looking at a guy in a pair of dress slacks and button-up shirt seated in the back with a brunette. His gaze flicked over to our table while I was still looking at him and his eyebrows drew down, his lips forming a thin line until he turned his attention back to the woman.

"Who is that?" I asked.

Jackie was still staring at him with an intensity I hadn't seen—even when she'd been pissed with me before. "My friend Chloe's ex, the one she found drilling his secretary on his desk one night. You might remember the tramp he cheated with. She's the one who bid on you at the auction."

That rankled me. Was that the only reason she'd decided to bid on a date with me? To shove the dagger into some woman who had wronged her friend? Heat filled my face, and I clenched my jaw.

"What's the matter with you?" Jackie asked, frowning at me.

"Nothing."

Her look told me I was full of shit. "Nice try."

Fine. She asked for it. "Is that why you bid on me?" I accused.

Her mouth fell open. "Are you serious?"

"As a heart attack."

Jackie blinked rapidly a few times. "After what happened the night of our date, you actually care how it came to be that I ended up there?"

"I do." I leaned forward over the table. "Now answer me and stop avoiding the question."

She huffed out a breath. "Is it one of the reasons? Yes. But it's not the only one."

"Explain." I crossed my arms over my chest like I did when I was working and trying to intimidate someone into telling me the truth.

"A big part of it was that I happen to think a lot of that charity, and they do so much good in the community." She crossed her arms over her chest and raised a brow, daring me to call her a liar.

I believed her, especially after what she'd told me about her father. The charity helped families who had lost a cop or firefighter in the line of duty.

"I wish they had had something like that when my father passed away." Jackie gave a sad smile.

I arched a brow. "And...what was the other part?"

Her eyes darted down to the tabletop.

"Jackie..."

"I wasn't about to let that tramp get her claws into you, okay?" she said in a heated voice.

A slow grin spread across my face as I realized the reason behind her words. "You were jealous."

She looked affronted. "I was not!"

"Please. Admit it. You were green with envy."

She shot me a death glare across the table, and I laughed.

"This is a little like the pot calling the kettle black, you know," she huffed. "I seem to remember someone manhandling me into a back alley while I was on a date so he could physically accost me. Sound familiar?" A self-satisfied smirk spread across her gorgeous face.

"Touché." I lifted my beer and took a sip. "I didn't, nor do I, like the idea of another man's hands on you."

She looked somewhat satisfied by that. "Well, I didn't like the idea of that tart's hands all over you, either. And when I started thinking of all the things she'd probably want to do with you at the end of the date, it pissed me off and I bid before I could really think about it."

Her statement left me wanting to beam, but I needed to know one more thing for sure. "Do you regret it?"

She paused for a beat. "No."

I grinned wide again, happy that at least that much was true.

# Chapter Fourteen

## Jackie

After dinner, I invited Jamie back to my place for drinks. *Why did I do that?* I probably came off as needy and desperate when I was none of those things. But as the evening had been winding down, I began to hate the idea of going home alone.

That was new.

I couldn't recall ever really feeling that way before, other than on the anniversary of my dad's death and what would've been his birthday if had he still been alive.

His truck pulled in behind me in the driveway, and he followed me up to the house. I opened the door and threw my purse on the front hall table, making my way to the kitchen. "Can I get you something to drink?" I knew that if Jamie agreed to my suggestion, it in all likelihood meant that he would be staying the night, having had too much to drive home.

"Sure. Whiskey if you have it."

I bent over to retrieve the bottle from the cupboard I kept all my booze in. I was a party girl. I had almost everything on hand. I stopped mid-crouch, thinking about how I hadn't felt that much like a party girl these past few weeks. Giving my head a shake, I decided I'd examine that later.

"One whiskey coming right up. How do you want it?"

"On the rocks."

I glanced back to see him checking out the picture of my dad on the mantle. My gut twisted at the sight, and I inhaled a deep breath to steady myself. "Coming right up." I'd have the same. I could use a stiff something that was for sure. I rolled my eyes at myself as I poured the liquid amber over the ice. Something stiff was exactly why I was feeling needy and edgy in the first place.

"Here you go," I said with a smile as I came into the living room.

Jamie was sitting on my couch now, so I set the drink on a coaster on the coffee table and took a seat beside him.

He leaned forward to grab his drink and clinked it with mine. "Cheers."

"Cheers."

We maintained eye contact as we each took a sip, the whiskey burning a path down to my stomach, but I liked the feeling of it. It distracted me from the pulsing in my core at the way Jamie was looking at me. I remembered that look well from when we'd been at his house.

"I'm curious who that guy was that approached you at the bar."

I blinked, taken aback. From the look on his face, I'd thought he was going to lean forward and kiss me. I would've preferred that to the conversation we were about to have. "I told you, just some guy I know."

"I got the feeling it was a little more than that," he said through a clenched jaw.

I raised my eyebrows. "Are you jealous?" It was nice to throw his earlier words back at him.

"Perhaps," he admitted.

I chewed on my lip for a moment, though I didn't know why I was feeling hesitant about telling him. I'd always been a tell-it-like-it-is kind of girl, and I had nothing to be ashamed of. I was an adult and single—I was entitled to a little fun.

"He's just a guy I used to...get together with from time-to-time." I shrugged, adding to the 'it meant nothing' vibe of my words.

Jamie's silver eyes narrowed. "He was a booty call."

"Yes," I responded in a small voice, then took a sip of my drink quickly so that I didn't have to elaborate further.

"He's got some balls walking up to the table with me sitting there. When is the last time you..." His faced was flushed, and I glanced down to see that the hand not holding his drink was fisted.

"Not recently. He was in a relationship, but I'm guessing they must've broken up."

Jamie seemed even more irked. "Why wouldn't he assume you and I are in a relationship?"

I stared at him for a moment. "Because he knows I don't do relationships."

"Let me get this straight." He leaned in, pinning me with his stare. "You don't date cops, firefighters, EMT workers, *and* you don't do relationships in general, period."

It sounded a little ridiculous when he put it like that, but I wasn't ashamed. It made perfect sense to me. "Um...yeah. Pretty much."

He shook his head and muttered to himself. I could've sworn he'd said something along the lines of "I've got my work cut out for me."

Jamie set his drink back down on the coaster and stood abruptly. "I'll be right back." He stalked toward the door, his body language, telling me that he was a man on a mission, though I hadn't the first clue what it was.

"Ooo-kay," I said to myself as I sat there, waiting for him to return. A minute later he came back in, not holding anything in his hands, but he did set his car keys down on the foyer table.

He made quick work of the space between us, seeming to eat up the hardwood in a few steps. When he reached me, he held out his hand. I took it, delighting in the feel of our skin making contact—finally—even if it was only his hand. That hand alone had brought me a lot of pleasure in the past.

I stood in front of him, unsure of his mood until he leaned in and brought his lips to mine in a savage kiss. My nipples pebbled and heat flooded my core as one of his hands gripped my ass, pressing me into him, while the other brushed against the side of my breast. Jamie took ownership of the kiss and his clean, male scent surrounded me until I could've melted in a pool at his feet I was so hot for him.

One of his hands dove into my hair, and he pulled away. "Where's your bedroom?" he asked gruffly.

"Down the hall," I squeaked out, suddenly nervous from the intense vibe rolling off him. I searched his face for any indication of what he was planning, but came up empty.

"Let's go." He turned on his heel and pulled me behind him down the hall. The feeling of déjà vu flooded over me as I was reminded of the similarity to the time we'd met up by accident at the bar.

We reached my room, and he dropped my hand. His gaze roamed me up and down several times before it came to rest on my face. "Take your clothes off. Nice and slow," he commanded.

A shiver raced out from my center, through my entire body. I began with my leather sandals, content to make him wait. He knew it too because he grinned as I bent to undo the buckles. I slipped them off and then removed my bracelets from my wrists, walking over to my dresser to place them on top. I turned to face him and reached for the hem of my black silk tank, raising it over my head and letting it fall. I was wearing a black lace, strapless bra underneath, and Jamie sucked in a breath when it came into view.

I squeezed my thighs together, trying to find some kind of relief from my growing arousal. The look on his face...it was as if he wanted to devour me. The intensity of it should've scared me, but it didn't.

"Keep going," he ordered in a gravelly voice.

Placing my thumbs underneath the elastic waist of my long, peasant style skirt, I pushed it down my hips until it fell in a pool of fabric around my feet. I lifted one foot out, then the other and whisked it to the side, across the hardwood.

"It's almost a shame to have to take all that lace off so I can fuck you."

*Holy shit,* the way this man talked! Sign me up for sexual slavery.

My panties grew wetter, his words alone teasing the physical response from me. I reached behind and unclasped my bra, letting it flutter to the floor, then palmed my breasts in my hands, enjoying the sight of Jamie's cock growing stiffer underneath his pants. There was a deep satisfaction in knowing that I was the one to coax such a reaction from him.

As I continued to play with my breasts, he reached down, undid his button, and unzipped his pants. Then he reached down and stroked himself, his eyes growing more and more hooded.

I licked my lips, and he groaned, which made me laugh a little.

He gave me a smirk. "Oh, you like that you drive me batshit crazy, do you?"

I gave him a saucy shrug and began pushing my panties down my legs. When they reached the floor, I kicked the scrap of lace fabric away.

"Now get on the bed." Carnal desire flickered in his eyes. "Lay on your stomach," he ordered.

I couldn't follow his instructions fast enough. I was desperate for him to touch me. My sex was pulsing with need, and my breasts felt weighted and heavy. I wanted his hands on me, in me—everywhere.

I crawled across my floral bedspread and lay on my stomach.

"Put your hands over your head and hold on to the headboard."

I did as he asked, the painted iron railings cold underneath my hands. I felt him get on the bed, the weight of him causing the mattress to dip. He crawled up along my left side and, before I knew what he was doing, cold metal was wrapping around my wrist.

*What the hell?*

My head whipped up to see that he'd cuffed my left wrist to the headboard. I turned my head further to find him looking down at me with so much intensity, it was almost too much to take.

"Do you trust me?" he asked, his gaze unwavering.

My chest constricted, my mouth suddenly parched. What a loaded question. And he knew it. I inhaled a deep breath, realizing that I wasn't sure when I had last given someone my trust. For me, the request was huge. Not only was he asking me to trust that he wouldn't do something to hurt me himself, but the bigger question being left unsaid was did I trust the universe enough to believe it wasn't going to screw me over again and take away something I cared for. Some*one* I care for.

I looked deep into his gray eyes, focusing on the green streaks in the middle and searching for the answer deep within me. For some reason, alarm bells weren't going off. I didn't feel the urge to run. I didn't want to push him away.

The truth was I did trust this man. As difficult as that was for me.

I nodded once, unable to voice the words out loud.

Jamie knew, though. He knew what a concession it was on my part that I'd even given him that much because a smile spread across his face, followed quickly by a wicked gleam in his eyes.

He leaned over to reach for my right wrist, the scent of soap and man following him, and I breathed in deep. God, his smell alone left me antsy with need.

Jamie clamped the second pair of cuffs to my other wrist and then to the iron railing. Apparently, he'd come prepared. I suppose there were some benefits to dating a police officer that I hadn't thought of before.

My forehead was resting against the comforter, unable to hold my neck at such an awkward angle anymore. The mattress shifted, and I pictured Jamie sitting back on his haunches, gazing down at me. There was no movement or sound for a minute, and I wanted to try and squirm my way out of the handcuffs with what I knew was his blatant perusal of my body. I didn't move, though, knowing he wanted me as badly as I wanted him.

I heard the rustle of fabric, and I assumed he was unbuttoning his shirt. I pictured his chiseled chest being revealed inch by glorious inch, and I opened and closed my hands, wishing I could see him, touch him, feel his skin under my fingertips. The mattress shifted again, then lifted. Jamie was off the bed now.

I pushed my forehead into the comforter more forcefully, growing impatient and wanting him inside of me. His boots clunked as he took each of them off, and I finally heard the telltale sign that his jeans were off when I heard the belt buckle clank against the hardwood floor. An image of his erection springing free, large and proud, assaulted my mind, and my clit throbbed with need.

When I turned my head to the side to say something sassy to him the words fell from my mind. He was there—standing at the side of the bed with his hand wrapped around the base of his cock. He began stroking himself while his gaze raked over my naked body. Wetness pooled between my thighs and I grew more impatient. There was something so carnal and hedonistic about watching him pleasure himself.

I squirmed, the cool metal of the handcuffs clanking against the headboard and cutting into my skin. "Jamie, please."

"Please what?" Amusement rang through in his voice.

"I want you to touch me. I need to feel your skin on me."

He smirked and stopped stroking, instead climbing onto the bed. "Lucky for you, I need to feel you right now, too." He came up over me and sat with each of his legs on either side of my ass. "You are so perfect, Jackie. Absolutely flawless."

I wasn't sure about that, but the adoration in his voice was hard to miss.

He leaned down and pressed his lips to the bottom of my spine and trailed a path of openmouthed kisses up to my neck. I wanted so badly to turn over so I could see him and take in his manly beauty.

Finally, his hard cock pressed into the crease of my

ass, and I lifted it in invitation. I wanted him inside me—desperately. I felt Jamie grin as he trailed another path of kisses down my body.

"I want to bury myself in you, Jackie. I need it rough right now. Can you handle rough?" He palmed one of my ass cheeks and squeezed.

I was practically panting now. I thought I might lose my mind if he didn't relieve the tension that had every part of my body in a stranglehold. "Rough sounds perfect." I wanted him to lose control, and I wanted to be the reason he had.

His finger dipped between my legs, and he groaned loudly. "You're drenched. That's so fucking hot." Placing both hands on my waist, he pulled me up so I was on my knees, my face pushing into the mattress, my ass high in the air.

Jamie stroked my center with his cock, brushing the tip over my engorged clit and back to my slit. I moaned and squirmed back and forth. "Damn it, Jamie. This is torture."

Without responding, he positioned himself over my entrance and thrust in until he filled me completely. I cried out in relief, arousal, and the feeling of suddenly being so full of him. He didn't give me any time to recover as he pulled out and slammed back into me, over and over again. He gripped my waist for leverage and was in no way gentle or loving. This was all about savage need and staking his claim over my body, and I was only too happy to let him do it.

My orgasm built, the pressure becoming almost too much as Jamie's pants and grunts came from behind me. He smacked my ass, and the stinging sensation rippled down to my sex in the most satisfying way. I cried out, and he did it again. And again.

I whipped my head back and forth on the bed so

overwhelmed by the sensations pummeling my body I could barely handle it, then Jamie's hands left my waist, and he stretched out over top of me, using his body weight to push me flat against the mattress. He stilled, his cock fully inside me, and pushed my legs together. When he slid out of me and back in, it was the most intense and blissful sensation that had ever rocked my body.

I bit into my lip as his powerful strokes between my legs sent me into an ecstasy I didn't even know existed. I screamed his name and clenched around his cock. Jamie finished with my name on his lips, both of us finding our release within seconds of each other.

After, he lay on top of me, catching his breath for a minute, and I didn't even care that his body weight was so heavy because I was utterly spent. Eventually Jamie reached for a key I hadn't noticed on the nightstand and released me from the handcuffs. He wrapped an arm around my waist, shifting us so we were spooning on our sides, his semi-hard erection still inside me.

"I should go clean up," I whispered.

He held me tighter. "No," he said, his voice raspy. "I want to fall asleep just like this. Me inside you."

I paused, unsure what to make of his request before I found that I really didn't want to move either. And so I fell asleep in the arms of a man for the first time ever.

# Chapter Fifteen

## Jackie

I was waiting in my chair on the front porch when Jamie pulled into my driveway. Nervous anticipation had my stomach feeling funny. It'd been a few days since we'd been able to line up our schedules, and today we'd planned to head to Sand Beach in Acadia National Park since it was supposed to be such a gorgeous summer day.

I smiled as I approached his vehicle, my beach bag in hand, already appreciating the white graphic T-shirt he had on. He had one arm hanging out the open window and gave me a small wave. I went around to the passenger side of the truck and climbed up in.

"Hey," I said giddily, bouncing myself into the seat. I wasn't able to deny the forward leap my feelings for Jamie had taken since we'd spent the night together.

Jamie leaned in and gave me a quick kiss on the cheek, but it still caused my heart to pick up speed. "It's good to see you," he said.

I gave him a shy smile.

"Do you mind if we swing by my dad's house on the

way? I called him before I left, and he didn't pick up. It's probably fine, but..." He was trying to play it off, but I didn't miss the hint of worry in his eyes.

"Of course. Whatever you need."

"Thanks, babe." He reached across the cab of the truck and squeezed my knee. That simple moniker set the butterflies fluttering in my chest.

There was something so normal, so domestic, about the small show of affection, but I wasn't used to it and my reaction took me by surprise. Was this what I'd been missing by swearing off relationships and deep feelings? I suspected it had more to do with Jamie himself and less with the fact that I was actually letting myself really feel for the first time.

A few minutes later, we rolled up into the driveway of a cute two-story home close to downtown. Jamie parked the truck and removed the key from the ignition, turning his body to face mine. "Want to come in?"

I blinked a couple times. "Do *you* want me to come in?" I asked, the emphasis on 'you'.

"I'd like that, yeah." He gave me a small smile, then got out of the truck. We walked hand-in-hand up the stone pathway. When we reached the door, Jamie gave it a quick knock and entered. I followed behind.

The home was cute in the way that older people's homes are. Family pictures everywhere, a traditional-looking sofa, and lots of knick-knacks on tables. I had to assume that they had been his mother's. The furniture was traditional and older, reminiscent of Maine decor and featuring hunter green fabric with floral covering one of the armchairs.

"Dad!" Jamie yelled out. "Dad, you here?" He waited a beat. When no answer came, he turned back to me. "Maybe he's out back. Come on."

We rushed into the kitchen to a sliding glass door

off the breakfast area when the sound of a tap running full blast caused each of us to stop. There was a glass set next to the kitchen sink and the tap was running, but no one was around. Jamie marched over to it and turned it off. When he turned back around, I noticed the crease in his forehead and knew he was concerned. He didn't say anything as he opened up the sliding glass door and stepped out onto a large deck, me following behind.

The yard was lovely with a nicely manicured lawn and large flowerbeds dotting the landscape. An elderly man stood staring at us from about halfway across the lawn, a look of confusion on his weathered face.

"Dad, are you okay?" Jamie rushed down the steps, while I chose to stay on the deck and give him some privacy. I wasn't sure what kind of situation we were walking in to.

They spoke for a couple minutes, his dad not even turning to direct his attention to Jamie. It was hard to tell from this distance but it seemed like maybe he was staring at me.

After a bit, they both made their way back to the deck, Jamie with his arm around his dad's shoulder. When they reached me, Jamie introduced us. "Dad, this is Jackie. Jackie, this is my father, Denny."

I gave a small wave since I wasn't close enough to shake his hand. "Hi, Denny. It's good to meet you."

"Betty, is that you?" he said with a dazed look.

My gaze darted to Jamie. I wasn't sure what to say or who Betty was.

Jamie turned to his dad. "No, Dad. This is Jackie. I just introduced you." His dad mumbled something unintelligible, and Jamie patted his shoulder. "I'll go get us some drinks. Dad, you need to make sure you have your hat on if you're going to be out here working in the garden. How long have you been standing out here? Your face is

ELISABETH GRACE

already burnt."

"I dunno," his father grumbled. "I don't even know whose place this is. Why did you bring me here?"

Jamie sighed. "Why don't you two have a seat at the table and I'll be right back. Lemonade okay for everyone?"

"Sounds good," I said, giving him an encouraging smile.

I walked over to the glass table and pulled out a chair, gesturing for Denny to have a seat. The slightly rusted table was covered by an umbrella, shading the area. He nodded stingily, and I took the chair directly across from him.

Denny sat in his seat and, before Jamie left to get our drinks, he leaned down and whispered in my ear from behind. "If it happens again and he thinks you're my mom, it's easiest to go along with it. Otherwise he might get agitated."

I nodded, my heart cracking a bit. I wondered how many times Jamie's dad had mistaken him for someone he wasn't and Jamie had been forced to play along.

I heard the sliding door close behind me. I wasn't exactly sure what to say, so I tried to make polite conversation. "You have a lovely yard here." A large magnolia tree stood proud in the corner of the yard, while a flower bed full of colorful variations of blooms followed along the fence line.

Denny's gaze sprung up to me. "Well, you should know, Betty. You're the one that done all the work."

I gulped, the casing around my heart fracturing a little more. "That's true, I suppose. So what do you think of the weather we've been having? We've really lucked out. Not much rain this summer."

To my surprise, his dad launched into an explanation of the clouds in the sky that day and why the weather patterns had led to such a nice summer. Before he had finished, Jamie returned and set a glass in front of each of us, taking the seat beside me.

"How's everything going?" he asked me warily.

"Great." I hoped my smile was reassuring.

Jamie nodded, though his lips were pressed together. "What have you been up to all day, Dad?"

"What am I a child?" he asked, irritated. "You think you have to check up on me and know what I'm doing every minute of the day? You remember who the father is here."

I kept my face smooth. I knew abrupt mood swings could occur in people with Alzheimer's, though it was more common in people with dementia. I wondered if it was possible that was what was going on. His demeanor earlier had been so sweet and instinct told me that had been the real Denny.

"Just making conversation, Dad," Jamie replied sadly.

Denny swung his head in my direction. "Can you believe this, Betty? Who does this boy think he is?"

"Now, Denny, just relax," I said in a soothing voice. "Your dad was just telling me all about cumulous clouds," I told Jamie.

"That's right," Denny jumped in before Jamie had a chance to respond. "I was explaining why we've been having such great weather this summer." He launched into the explanation again, and I was happy to listen to it all a second time. A deep satisfaction hit me, too, at the look of pleasure on Jamie's face while his dad spoke.

When he was finished, he was quiet and sunk back into his chair. I reached for my cup and took a drink, drawing Denny's attention back to me.

"Well, are you going to introduce me to your friend or not?" Denny asked Jamie.

Jamie appeared startled for a second, but quickly

composed himself. "Dad, this is Jackie. Jackie, this is my dad, Denny."

This time I leaned forward over the table to shake his hand. "Pleasure to meet you."

He took my hand in his. "The pleasure is all mine." Raising his eyebrows at Jamie, he said, "You better not screw this one up, son. She's a real beaut."

We both laughed, and Jamie actually seemed to relax a little, much to my delight.

"He's never brought anyone over to meet me, you know. I'd say that bodes well for you."

I laughed again, amused by his candor. "Well," I leaned forward over the table and lowered my voice as if we were sharing a secret of our own, "I'll be sure not to do something to screw it up then." I winked.

Denny leaned back in his chair, laughing heartily. When I glanced over at Jamie, he was looking between the two of us, in awe.

"So what do you do for a living, Jackie?" Denny asked me. I went on to explain my job. "That where you and Jamie met then?" He picked up his lemonade and drank a sip.

"Not exactly," I said, a rueful smile on my face.

Jamie smirked. "I came across Jackie with a flat on the side of the road one day when I was on duty," Jamie said.

"And he was a complete pompous ass," I added.

Denny laughed and leaned forward, squeezing the hand I had resting on the table. "I like you, sweetheart. You seem like you can put this boy in his place." He nodded over to Jamie.

"I don't need anyone to put me in my place, dad." Jamie grinned and shook his head.

"Oh hogwash." His dad waved a wrinkled, bony hand. "It would be good for you."

I giggled and turned to Jamie in time to see him roll his eyes. "Whatever you say, dad."

We stayed a while longer until Jamie rose from the table, announcing that we had to be on our way.

His dad stood to see us off. "It was a pleasure to meet you, Jackie. I do hope I'll see you again soon."

"Thanks. Same to you, Mr. McTavish."

"It's Denny, remember?" He took my hand and patted it, a warm smile on his face.

"Right. I'm sorry."

Jamie took his dad in a fierce embrace, smacking his back until they pulled away from each other. "I'll stop by after my shift tomorrow."

"Okay. See you then." He patted Jamie's cheek. The tender gesture left me with a brief melancholy feeling, wishing that my own father were still around to do the same to me.

"Ready?" Jamie asked me.

I swallowed, pushing down the ache that accompanied the memory of my dad. "Ready."

We headed back through the house and out to the truck.

"Your dad sure seemed to know a lot about the weather."

Jamie stuck the keys in the ignition and started the truck, turning the air conditioner to high. "He used to be a weatherman. Studied meteorology at school."

"That's so cool. I've never met an actual weatherman before."

Jamie smiled, though it looked a little sad. He grew quiet after that, seeming to contemplate something. "I'm glad my dad had a lucid moment there and was able to meet you." He leaned across, placing one hand on my cheek and kissed my lips. He held his lips there for a moment, and the weight of the emotion behind the kiss

ELISABETH GRACE

was not lost on me.

"I'm happy I was able to meet him," I said with sincerity.

"I'm glad to know that even when he does go into his own world, and if he never comes out of it, that somewhere in there is a memory of you. Even if he can't recognize it."

The air pushed out of my lungs. This man was such a surprise. I'd learned that, even though Jamie was demanding and an entirely different creature in the bedroom, outside of it he was a gentle soul who felt deeply.

For me.

That was the part that amazed me the most.

# Chapter Sixteen

## JAMIE

I carried the small cooler I'd packed along with my bag as Jackie and I made our way over the warm sand to find a spot not already taken by the substantial crowd. Apparently, the blue skies and sunshine had given a bunch of people the same idea as us.

"How about here?" Jackie turned to me, the ocean breeze blowing her hair in front of her face.

"Looks as good as any." I set everything down on the sand, watching Jackie pull a colorful beach towel from her bag and spread it out.

I'd known instantly upon meeting her that there was something special about her, but I never would've guessed, based on our first meeting, what a phenomenal woman she would end up being. The way she had interacted with my dad today—with compassion and patience as he'd rambled on or thought that she was my mother—had only endeared me to her further. I knew from her profession that she took her civic duty of helping others as seriously as I did, but what today had made clear to me was that it was just a part of her that wanted to help those in need.

"Jamie." She cocked her head at me. "Everything okay?"

I didn't realize I'd been staring out at the ocean, lost to my memories. "Yeah, everything's great." I stepped over to her, gripping the back of her neck and bringing her in for a fierce kiss, bystanders be damned. By the time we'd pulled away from each other, Jackie's eyes were hooded and full of need.

"Save that thought for later," I said and chucked her chin.

She laughed. "You shouldn't start something you can't finish."

I bent to grab my towel from my bag. "Ha. Don't tempt me. You remember what happened the last time I saw you in a bikini? There were people floating around then too, and it didn't stop me." I gave her a wicked grin, and she laughed as she tugged her tank top off, tossing it into her bag, her shorts following right behind.

She was wearing a different bikini than the one she'd worn at Don's retirement party, though she looked just as good. This one was primarily white with black trim and a bright Aztec pattern. Her tone, tanned body was on display and, as I glanced around, I realized I wasn't the only one appreciating her beauty. That was okay. I wasn't some prick that couldn't stand other men checking out his woman...though I wasn't even sure I could call her that yet. Sure, we'd slept together a couple times, but that seemed to be Jackie's MO. I hadn't broached the subject of exactly what was happening between us because I feared forcing Jackie to put a label on it might end it.

Jackie lay down on her stomach, and I took the spot beside her on my own towel, laying on my back and propping myself up on my elbows. "This is a nice beach."

Sand Beach, as it was called, was an inlet of sorts surrounded by large chunks of rock cropping up and forming a hill where a lush forest grew on top. The two points of land stretched out farther into the ocean than the inlet beach, giving it a private feel, even though the sandy shoreline was peppered with people.

She lifted up and set her hands on her chin. "Is this your first time here?"

"Yeah, I came into Acadia once on my own for a hike, but I didn't see this part."

"I hope you brought your bear spray," Jackie laughed.

I raised an eyebrow. "I was smart enough to talk to one of the Rangers to see what essentials I needed to bring." I tapped the side of my head and grinned. "Not as dumb as I look."

A sexy smile broke out on Jackie's face. "Oh, I wouldn't say you look dumb."

I leaned toward her a bit. "What would you say?"

She laughed again and shook her head. "Oh no. You are not sucking me into saying something that'll feed your ego."

I couldn't help but laugh. Jackie always seemed to be of the opinion that my ego was out of control.

We both lay there for a while, soaking in the sunshine. Yes, the sun was bad for you. But when you lived in a state that only got summer three months of the year, you were going to enjoy the heat to the fullest while you could.

"Did you want something to eat or drink? I packed some fruit and water," I said when the heat began getting to me.

Jackie pulled her head up off the towel and squinted at me. "Water would be great, thanks."

I nodded and sat up, reaching for the cooler and pulling a pair of water bottles out, handing one to Jackie. She stretched her neck up so she could drink it while still laying on her front. She looked so sexy lying there, I had to fight the urge to lean in and run my tongue along a path straight to her earlobe.

When we'd both had our fill—of water—I returned the bottles to the cooler to keep them cold.

"Do you think you could rub some lotion on my back?" She pushed her sunglasses up onto her head for a second, revealing her bright green eyes. "I put some on before I left the house, but it's starting to get really hot."

"I'd rather rub it on your front," I said, wagging my eyebrows.

Jackie rolled her eyes, looking exasperated with my one track mind, and reached into her bag for the suntan lotion. I took it from her and half crawled over her back so that I was straddling her just below her ass. Squirting some of the lotion into my hand, I closed the lid again and dropped it on my towel. I rubbed my hands together for a second and then wasted no time rubbing the liquid into the soft skin on her back. I tried really hard to think of something other than ripping Jackie's bikini off of her.

Then Jackie said, "It must be really hard for your dad when he comes out of an episode."

Well, that would do it.

"Does he realize afterward what happened?"

I heaved a sigh. "Not usually, but sometimes, if he realizes he's missing time, then he assumes that's what happened."

"That's tough. On him and you."

I know she'd lost her father as a child and that brought its fair share of pain to her life, but it was a particular kind of agony having to watch a parent suffer and unravel before your eyes. "Yeah. I think I'm going to have to have the nurse come by more often to keep an eye on him." Shifting myself farther down so I could rub the lotion on the back of her legs, I tried to concentrate on that, not wanting to delve too deeply into the subject matter. We were here to enjoy ourselves. " I can't be there as much as I'd like, and I need to know if his episodes are becoming more frequent." I dragged my hand down Jackie's firm leg, making sure she was thoroughly protected from the sun.

"You must really love your dad. A lot of people would've stuck him in a home as soon as they got the diagnosis."

She was right about that, but I couldn't bring myself to do it. He'd supported me my entire life and it was time for me to do the same for him. "He was a wonderful father. I was lucky. Not everyone gets that. It was worth giving up everything I had in Boston to be here to help him." I eased up off of Jackie's towel and went back to lay on my own, choosing to lay on my stomach this time.

Jackie and I had both turned our heads so we were looking at each other. "What or who did you have to give up?" she asked softly, a slight hesitation in her voice.

"No 'who'," I assured her. "But I was aiming for S.W.A.T., and I was close to getting it." I almost winced at the memory of exactly how close I'd been. "I had to leave that dream behind to move here."

Every muscle in Jackie's body seemed to tense at my words. "Your dream is to be on the S.W.A.T. team?" Her eyes were big now, anxiously awaiting my response.

"It was. Like I said, I had to leave it behind in Boston."

She looked unconvinced. "People don't just give up on their dreams that easily."

I pressed my lips into a thin line. "I suppose not...maybe someday it'll happen for me, but for now my dad has to be my priority."

Jackie bit her lip, looking thoughtful for a moment.

"Hey, what is it?" I asked, concerned I'd said something wrong.

She smiled up at me, the cloud in her eyes clearing. "It's nothing." Rolling over onto her back, she sat up. "Want to go take a dip in the water?"

"Think it'll be warm?" I asked, rolling onto my back and sitting up, too.

Jackie shrugged. "Warm enough."

I stood up and stretched a hand down to help her up. She took it and adjusted her bikini once she was standing.

"Alright. I don't want any shrink dink happening. I've got a woman to impress, you know." I wagged my eyebrows, grinning wide.

She laughed. "Well, you should know she's more than impressed with your dink. No worries there." She winked.

I puffed my chest out in mock pride. "Happy to hear it."

"Geez, you're making me wish the water was freezing. You could do with a cold bucket of water over your head."

I laughed and draped my arm across her shoulders as we began the trek over the sand to the water's edge.

There were things to miss about Boston, to be sure, but it had never felt as much like home as these past few weeks with Jackie had.

# Chapter Seventeen

## Jackie

I banged on Chloe's door later that night, restless and tired of pacing around my own house. Her kid sister, Jess, ended up answering.

"Hey, Jess. Is your sister in?"

She smiled big. "Yep. She's in the kitchen, cleaning up after dinner. I'm headed out to meet some friends for a bit, so I'll see you later." She sailed past me, giving me a small wave and bounding off the porch.

"Chlo!" I called as I walked in and closed the door behind me.

"In the kitchen," she called.

I entered her country kitchen to find her drying dishes beside the sink, so I plopped myself in a chair at the breakfast table. "Hey, babe. You might want to consider putting a chastity belt on Jess. She's turning into quite the looker."

Chloe's shoulders slumped, and she turned to face me. "Don't I know it. I can't believe she's going to be done with high school in a couple years. It's gone so fast."

I gave her contemplative nod, thinking of my father who I'd lost years before Chloe's mother had been killed. "Time marches on."

"That it does," she said, setting the dish towel on the counter. "I was about to make a tea. Would you like one?"

I twirled a piece of hair around my finger. "Do you have anything stronger?"

"Uh-oh. That can't be good." She came to sit across from me at the table. "What's going on?"

I hunched down in the chair and crossed my arms over my chest. "Jamie's going on, that's what."

She frowned. "I don't understand. Last I heard from you, you guys were seeing each other and doing the horizontal mambo. What happened?"

I huffed. "He wants to be S.W.A.T., Chlo. It's his dream. He had to leave it behind when he moved here to help his dad."

Chloe leaned forward and looked at me like she was waiting for more.

"S.W.A.T.!" How did she not get how awful this was? "Those are the guys they send in when things really go to shit."

She shrugged. "Okay, well he's not on it right now, so what's the problem?"

I leaned forward with my arms out to the side. "The problem is that it's his dream. I already had major reservations about seeing him because he was a cop, and now I find out he wants to do one of the most dangerous cop jobs there is. It's too much for me!" I threw my hands up in the air, feeling defeated and awful. I couldn't imagine giving Jamie up now, but then...I couldn't deal with it if he needed S.W.A.T. I needed security. Being a cop was risky enough. And I wasn't yet sure I was even able to deal with that.

Chloe looked like she was working something out in her head for a second, which was her way so I let her do it. She got up and filled the kettle, placed it on the stove, and turned the burner to high. "Jackie, I love you, but you're making no sense. So what if some day far in the future he decides to join the S.W.A.T. team?" She was quiet for another moment and then a look of realization broke across her features, and she walked slowly back to her seat. "Unless what you're feeling for him makes you think this is something long term." The look of excitement in her eyes was bubbling higher by the second.

Whoa. Whoa. Backup the bus. "That is not what this is about."

"Are you sure?" she asked, totally serious. What had my friend been smoking?

"You can't fall in love with someone that quickly," I snapped.

"Says who?" she fired back.

"I don't know...everyone!"

Chloe leaned back into her seat with her arms crossed. "Okay then. Tell me, wise one, exactly how long does it take someone to fall in love?"

I stared at her, unable to answer. I had no idea. Was there a right answer? A wrong one? And who decided? Finally, I let out a sound of frustration.

A smile spread across Chloe's face. "I love it when I'm right."

"You're not right," I argued, clenching my hands in my lap.

"Maybe I'm not." She held her hands up in a gesture of peace. "Maybe you're not in love with him—yet. But the only reason this whole S.W.A.T. thing would bother you is if your feelings for him are strong enough that you think he'll be around for a while." She pinned me a look that dared me to disagree. My mouth hung open and silent for a long moment. I got lucky when the kettle started whistling on the stove, and she had to break eye contact.

"Maybe you're right about that," I said begrudgingly.

Chloe finished making her tea and returned to sit with me at her breakfast table.

"How are you feeling about that? If I know you, right about now you're panicking inside  realizing how deep your feelings are for this guy."

I sighed. "Funny enough, I don't feel panicked. But that doesn't mean I can do this." I didn't know if I was capable of the leap of faith being with Jamie would require.

Chloe leaned forward and reached for my hand. "A word of advice?" I nodded for her to continue. "Just enjoy whatever time you've got with him. You might as well. If it's destined to end, wouldn't it be better to spend the present living in the moment rather than worrying about what could happen? I guarantee if anything ever did happen, you'd only kick yourself for not enjoying it while it lasted."

God, she sounded just like Jamie. How had I ended up with all these deep thinkers in my life? Me, the girl that didn't want to feel or think too deeply about anything.

I narrowed my eyes at her. "I really hate when you're right."

Chloe laughed. "Funny, I love it."

I shook my head at her and rolled my eyes. She did have a point. I'd let Chloe into my heart and look how that had turned out. Now I couldn't imagine not having her in my life. Maybe some people were worth the risk.

# Chapter Eighteen

## JAMIE

I reached down to the middle of the cruiser and grabbed my water bottle to take a sip. One of the downsides of no longer being in Boston was that coffee and donuts were not readily available during a nightshift. At least it was a quiet night. I was a little outside of town, driving the back roads and making the rounds to ensure there wasn't anyone up to no good. The only thing around here were country homes, a lot of grass, and the occasional field of blueberries. Only a couple more hours and the sun would be up, then I'd be able to crash at home.

As I drove past a small, rundown restaurant at the side of the road, I scanned the parking lot and interior of the building to be sure there was no activity. The radio crackled, making me think of Jackie. We'd found our shifts overlapping a handful of times over the past few weeks, but I wouldn't get to hear her voice tonight. She had the night off and would be tucked into bed, fast asleep.

A deep voice came over the line. "We have a report of a carbon monoxide alarm going off at seven-sixty-three Maple Avenue in Bar Harbor. Neighbor called it in. Fire and paramedics are on route."

*Seven-sixty-three Maple?*

The feeling of ice crawled over my skin, slowing the blood in my veins. Numb, I picked up the radio to respond. "Ten Four. This is ninety-nine, thirty-four. Can you repeat that address?"

"Seven-six-three Maple Avenue."

*Fuck. Fuck, fuck.* That was Jackie's place.

I responded to the operator and turned my lights and siren on, not caring that the operator hadn't used a Code Four, giving me permission. Nothing was going to slow me from getting to her.

I raced across the country roads with my high beams on, praying no wildlife jumped out in front of me. My stomach was twisted in knots, my heart pounding in my chest until it was the only thing I could hear. All I could picture was Jackie lying in bed and drifting off, unknowingly suffocating while she slept.

"Fuck!" I slammed the heel of my hand against the steering wheel. No, if the neighbor called she must not be home to hear it. Unless...

The journey back into town felt never ending, and I was frustrated as hell that I couldn't get there fast enough.

Finally, I squealed around the corner of her street. The fire truck was already parked in front of her house, and my heart dropped even further into my stomach. I'd come upon scenes like this more times than I could count, but not one of them had ever filled me with the sense of dread that seeing the spinning lights from the fire engine reflecting off her house did.

I slammed the car to a stop behind the red beast, threw it in park, and rushed up the driveway. An older woman was standing on the driveway next door, a worried expression marring her face while she clutched her robe closed. A couple of firemen were banging on the door and another was making his way around the side of the house to the back of the bungalow. Jackie's car was in the driveway, which sent my stomach into a free fall. Bile rose up into my throat.

The entire ride over, I'd been hopeful that she would be out—even though that meant she'd be out in the middle of the night, doing God knows what, with God knows who. It was still better than the alternative.

I took the porch steps two at a time. "What's the story?" I asked frantically.

Chris, a firefighter I recognized but didn't know well, turned to face me. "Neighbor said she woke up to go to the bathroom and heard something through her open window. She listened for a few minutes and finally figured out that it was a $CO_2$ detector alarm coming from this house. We've banged a couple times, but no one answered."

*Bang! Bang! Bang!* The other guy slammed his fist against the door. "This is the fire department. Please come to the door."

"Fuck this guys," I yelled, frustrated and panicked. "This is Jackie *Davenport*'s place. Just take the fucking door down."

Chris whipped his head in my direction. "Jackie, the nine-one-one operator?"

"Yeah, now get the fucking door down!"

"God damn." He turned to the other firefighter by his side. "Let's do this." He lifted his foot to give the door a good kick by the lock and handle when it all of a sudden whipped open.

There stood Jackie, in a tank top and boy short underwear, eyes wide, all color drained from her face. "What the hell?"

Chris dropped his foot to the porch just in time to not give Jackie what would've been a very painful kick in the stomach.

Her gaze ping-ponged between all of us before

finally settling on me. "What's going on?"

Relief swept through me swift and sure, almost bringing me to my knees. I didn't give a shit who was around. I pushed between the other guys, moving them out of the way, and pulled Jackie forcefully into my chest, wrapping her in my arms. I needed to feel her against me, to know that she was alive and well.

"Thank God you're okay." I kissed the top of her head, squeezing my eyes shut.

"I don't understand what's happening," she mumbled against me.

"Your $CO_2$ alarm was going off—there was no smoke or anything, but your neighbor heard the alarm, and she figured out what it was and called it in. When you didn't answer, we thought..." I swallowed past the enormous lump in my throat. "Fuck, I can't even say it." I squeezed her tighter, not caring that it probably made her uncomfortable.

After a few moments, a throat cleared behind me. "Jamie, we need to get in there to test the air quality and see if there's a problem," Chris said.

I reluctantly let Jackie step back from me. "Yeah, sure," I said, turning my head to address Chris. I looked back at Jackie, now doing a sweep of her from head to toe. "You sure you're okay?"

"I'm fine." She wrapped her arms around herself. "A little shaken at being woken up like this, but otherwise okay. I went to bed with ear plugs in because someone down the street was having a party."

She said she was fine, but I didn't miss the way her whole body shook slightly or how wide her eyes were.

"The ambulance is at the end of the driveway," Chris said. "You should let them give you a onceover."

Jackie glared over at him. "I'm fine."

Chris shook his head and then put his oxygen mask

over his face. "Suit yourself." He and the other guy entered the house.

I squeezed a hand around her shoulder. "Come on, you can wait in my squad car. I'll get you a blanket." It was a summer night, and she certainly wouldn't freeze to death, but I didn't want any of the guys here taking advantage of the situation and checking her out in the small amount of clothing she was wearing.

She nodded and took my hand before we made our way over to the car. A few of the firemen expressed their relief at seeing she was okay. I retrieved a blanket from my trunk, then wrapped it around her shoulders and brought her in for another embrace.

"Did you want to sit in the car?" I asked.

She shook her head. "I just want to stay here...in your arms."

Fine by me. I continued to hold her until she began shaking again, so I pulled her in tighter. I could hold her like this forever.

"Hey, are you cold?" I ran my hands up and down her back.

"No, I think...I...it's setting in what could've happened if my neighbor didn't call nine-one-one. I should go thank Mrs. Wilson."

I glanced up to the house. The pair of firefighters had just exited. "Sure, you do that while I talk to Chris and see what's going on."

Jackie nodded at me, blinking rapidly several times, and pulled the blanket tighter around her. She crossed the lawn in her bare feet, heading to her neighbor as I made my way up her driveway.

Chris met me halfway, heading to the fire truck from the house. "All the levels are normal. No $CO_2$ in there. Looks like it was a faulty detector." He shrugged. "It happens sometimes."

Well, thank God for that. At least Jackie hadn't been in any real danger. "Is she free to go back inside?"

"Yeah, just make sure to tell her to replace that thing tomorrow. I've unplugged it from the wall and removed the battery."

"Will do." I extended a hand, and he shifted the mask he'd been wearing to his other hand so he could shake mine. "Thanks so much."

"No thanks needed. You know as well as anyone it's what we do. Though if I'd realized it was Jackie's place, I probably would've knocked the door down after she didn't answer the first time." He gave a humorless laugh. "It would've been worth her wrath."

I gave him a small smile, not wanting to comment on the Wrath of Jackie. That could only get me in trouble. "Everything turned out okay, so it's all good."

Chris smiled back, then patted my shoulder as he walked past me.

Looking across to the other house, I saw Jackie hugging her neighbor and I squeezed my eyes shut for a moment. What would I have done if anything had happened to her? The truth—I have no fucking clue, but I would've been devastated. Suddenly, the depth of my feelings for this women hit me dead center and almost bowled me over. I would miss everything about her...her wit, her strength, her beauty—even her god damned stubbornness.

I returned to my cruiser to report back and, after seeing that it was only a half hour until I was off duty, I let the station know I'd be sticking around to make sure Jackie was okay, but that I'd have my radio on until the end of my shift.

I removed the keys from the ignition, having forgotten in my panic to do so when I'd first arrived. Jackie was already waiting for me on the front porch. "You alright?" I asked her. She appeared more put together now. Her color had returned to her cheeks and she was no longer shaking.

"I think so. Chris filled me in. I feel bad for Mrs. Wilson. I think she was more embarrassed than anything when she heard it was a false alarm."

I blinked at her, confounded. Jackie had to have been scared shitless by the possibility of what could've happened tonight, and yet she was more concerned about her neighbor. Would this woman ever cease to amaze me?

"She did the right thing," I said, pulling her into my arms again. I didn't want to stop touching her. The physical contact grounded me, let me know she was alive and okay. The thought of...

No, I couldn't go there. I couldn't even consider the possibility of my life without Jackie, of a world where she didn't exist. A few months ago, I hadn't even known her and now she was my whole world—she was the sun and I revolved around her.

"I told her the same thing," Jackie said softly.

I held her for a moment longer, then let her go. "Come on, let's get you back inside and tucked into bed." I brushed my knuckles against her cheek.

She closed her eyes and leaned into my hand. "Don't you have to finish your shift?"

"I'm off soon anyway, and I already called in and told them I wasn't leaving. There's another car on if anything should happen in the next—" I lifted my hand to glance at my watch. "—twenty minutes."

She placed her palm to my cheek and stroked it with her thumb. "Well then, take me to bed, Officer McTavish."

ELISABETH GRACE

# Chapter Nineteen

## Jackie

I was attempting to hold myself together in front of Jamie, but the truth was I was still a little shaken. Sure it had turned out to be nothing, but I couldn't help but be freaked out by the possibility. It was like if you went to the doctor and they told you that you had cancer and later said they'd made a mistake. Just because the worst hadn't actually happened didn't diminish the feelings you had when you thought you were in danger. I'd exhaled in relief when Jamie said he'd be staying—I didn't want to be alone.

Now, as we made our way down the hall to my bedroom, all I wanted was for him to make me feel safe, alive—loved. My room was dark since I hadn't wasted any time turning the light on when I'd heard the pounding at my front door.

When we reached my room Jamie walked toward me, his heavy footsteps echoing on the hardwood. He pushed a hand into my hair and cupped my head, gazing at me with such adoration it made me feel precious. Eventually he pulled me in for a kiss. Our tongues tangled at a slow, languid pace, tasting each other as he pressed me into his hard body.

After a moment, he pulled back and looked deep into my eyes, cupping my face in his hands. "When I thought something happened to you..." He trailed off and swallowed hard, unable or unwilling to finish his thought.

Jamie squeezed his eyes shut for a second, then dropped his forehead to my own. I breathed in his scent—pure, clean male—and my skin instantly tingled with arousal. He kissed me again, only breaking contact to pull my shirt up over my head. Wrapping his arms around me, he pulled me in close, nipping and sucking my lips and eventually tracing a path of slow openmouthed kisses down my neck and across my shoulders.

I felt cherished, loved, and alive. So alive. After what had happened I needed to lose myself in him.

He gently cupped both of my breasts in his palms, kneading them and flicking my nipples with the lightest of touches. I let out a breathy moan and reached for his waist, pulling his uniform shirt out from his pants. Bringing my fingers up to the top of his shirt, I backed away enough to watch for myself as I undid the buttons and revealed one-by-one the expanse of his defined chest. I placed my palms on his hard pecs and dragged them slowly up to his shoulders, pushing his shirt up and over until it fell down the length of his arms.

I suppressed a shiver as I took in his raw beauty. His body was perfection, but underneath the solid muscle and fuckable exterior was a man who possessed a heart bigger than anyone I'd ever known—a man who now possessed my soul.

Jamie's heavy lidded gaze told me how much he wanted me as well, but tonight was different. We wouldn't be fucking tonight. The weight of so many emotions hung in the air. Words were left unsaid, but not unfelt—at least not by our hearts.

I leaned forward and took his nipple into my mouth, flicking it with my tongue as I played with the waistband of his pants. His stomach muscles rippled and contracted in response, spurring me on further. I placed kiss after kiss on his heated skin, tracing a path until I circled his body and ended up behind him. I stood back for a moment, admiring the muscular planes of his back and the way the muscles moved as Jamie worked to remove his utility belt and unzip his pants.

Jamie stretched forward and placed his belt on the bedside table, then slid his pants and boxers down his legs. I circled my arms around his waist, enjoying the feel of his skin pressed against my breasts as I peppered his back with kisses. He turned, pushing his hands into my hair and staring down at me like he couldn't believe I was real.

"God, Jackie...I can't get enough of you." He leaned in and kissed my forehead. "It's never enough," he whispered.

I sighed as the overwhelming feeling of safety, security, and love enveloped me. But...did I really love this man or was I just caught up in the moment? Before I could ponder that thought too long, Jamie's hands slid down the side of my waist, causing a full body shiver. He dropped to his knees and gently slid my boy short underwear down my legs.

Taking my hand, he stood and led me to the bed. I lay in the middle and waited for him to join me. Crawling up the mattress and over top of me, he lowered himself just enough that I was able to feel his warm skin brush against me, but not enough to crush me. His lips found mine again, his tongue sweeping in and toying with my own, stoking the rising inferno inside of me. Heat pooled in my core as I ran my hands along the expanse of his back and squeezed his ass cheeks.

"We are so perfect together," he mumbled against

my lips. "Can't you see that?"

I simply nodded, unable to speak, the weight of my emotions crippling me. Love and adoration welled up inside of me, pushing the air from my lungs.

He slid down my body, stopping here and there to run his warm tongue along my over sensitized skin until he spread my legs open and splayed me before him.

"You are so perfect," he moved his gaze from my eyes to my bared center and back, "everywhere." Leaning in while still maintaining eye contact, he sucked and tongued my clit.

I watched as he made love to my pussy with his mouth. "Oh, Jamie," I moaned, pushing my hands into his hair.

His tongue movements were slow and drawn out for my pleasure, but not at all intended to bring me to release. I languished in that blissful space for what seemed like hours when he finally rose up. He wiped his chin with the back of his hand and moved back up my body. I wrapped my legs around him, needing him—needing to feel his hard length fill that empty space inside me.

He gazed down at me in awe and pushed in, closing his eyes as he did and I sighed. The feeling was so exquisite I wanted to remember it always. Not unlike his body filling mine, his presence in my life had filled a gaping wound that had been present for longer than I could remember.

Jamie pulled out slowly and rocked back into me. He carried on like this. While my green gaze held his gray one, the connection between us grew and the realization that we were making love, not fucking, seeped into my consciousness. This was different than any of the other times we'd been together. It was a good different.

The tingling between my legs grew, and I knew I wouldn't be able to hold off my orgasm much longer. Jamie's pace picked up a bit. Then, as I came, I cried out, prisms of light shooting across the back of my closed eyelids as my release pulsed through me. With a few sharp thrusts, Jamie groaned and emptied himself inside me.

Both of us were panting as Jamie lowered his forehead to mine, running the back of his knuckles across my cheek. "See how right we are together," he said softly.

I was so overwhelmed by emotion that I squeezed my eyes shut for a moment, unwilling or unable to see if the same feelings swam through his gaze, too.

Without another word, he pulled himself from me and cringed at the loss. Sliding back the covers, he motioned for me to get underneath them. I complied and he joined me, spooning me from behind and pulling me back into him.

We lay there, quiet. Well, the room itself was silent, but the voices in my head were beginning to roar as the post-orgasmic bliss faded. They were screaming at me, demanding to know what this meant, what exactly I felt for Jamie, and wondering how I could put myself in the position to once again lose someone who meant so much to me.

I tried to shut the voices out, but I'd already given them a foot in the door and they wouldn't retreat easily, so I lay there, restless and wide awake.

I fell asleep long after Jamie's breathing grew steady, still unsure whether allowing Jamie into my life was my biggest breakthrough or my biggest mistake.

ELISABETH GRACE

# Chapter Twenty

## Jackie

Ever since the night of the false alarm at my house, I'd been trying to maintain some distance from Jamie. We still spent time together and saw each other, but if he wanted to come in after we'd been out for a night, I'd make up an excuse about why I needed to get up early, or say that Chloe was stopping by in the morning.

What I'd felt the night we'd made love was still too intense for me to deal with. I couldn't—not with the anniversary of my father's death upon me. I dreaded this day every year. It wasn't as if it was any more painful this particular day of the year, but it was an agonizing reminder that time marches on. It brought to the surface that my dad hadn't seen all the changes in my life since the last anniversary. That he wouldn't ever walk me down the aisle, or see his grandchildren. Sometimes I wondered if that was another reason I tried to keep those types of milestones at such a distance.

This day made me feel like that scared little ten-year-old girl again, and I hated it. I hated feeling so weak when I'd spent every day since his murder erecting walls so that nothing could ever make me hurt that much or feel that fragile again.

As I drove through town, I readied myself to meet my mom at the cemetery. It had become our tradition every anniversary. I could only bear to visit his gravestone once a year, but I had my suspicions that my mom still went all the time.

The tall trees along the narrow cemetery road swayed in the warm breeze. By all accounts, it was a beautiful day. The sun was shining, there was barely a cloud in the sky, and the smell of the nearby ocean wafted in on the air. Yet all of this couldn't be more opposite of my mood.

My mom's car was already parked along the laneway, so I pulled in behind her and grabbed the flowers I'd purchased off the passenger seat. I was wearing ballet flats since I'd learned long ago that heels would only dig into the soft grass. Making my way up the slight incline, I saw my mom on her knees in front of Dad's gravestone. It was clear from the hunch and movement of her shoulders that she was crying.

I braced myself, not knowing what I would encounter this year. Some were better than others, but even so I was always required to be the rock. My mom was the one who got to fall apart.

I fell to my knees beside her, setting the flowers on the grass, and rubbed her back in small circles. "Hi, Mom."

"Oh, honey." She turned to her side and enveloped me in a hug, clinging to me while she sobbed on my shoulder. I hugged her back, my own tears springing to my eyes, but I fought to keep them under control. When my mom pulled away, she wiped under her eyes with a handkerchief that I recognized as one of my dad's. It had been passed down to him by his father long ago. "I'm sorry.

I'm sorry, honey. I know you hate this."

I sighed. Over the years I'd voiced my displeasure with my mom at her lack of being able to move on. It had always fallen on deaf ears, so I'd stopped saying anything.

"Mom, it's not that. I miss Dad, too." I reached for her hand and squeezed it, knowing too well that a piece of you was missing after losing someone you loved. "I just think at some point you have to choose to move on with your life—even though he's not in it." Tears built in my eyes. It was difficult to say, even more difficult to put into practice, but if we didn't what chance did we stand at living a happy existence?

She turned away from me, her shoulder-length bob swishing across her neck. Fidgeting and arranging the flowers I'd laid down, she took a moment before responding. "And how exactly am I supposed to do that? When I was the happiest I could ever be with him. And then it was all ripped away in a split second." She whipped her head around to face me again—anger, grief, and fear all swimming in her eyes, even after all this time.

Tears sprang to my eyes as I witnessed, once again, how much pain my mother was in. "I don't know, Mom. I really don't." I drew in a large breath, not sure whether I should say what I wanted to next. The last time I'd mentioned it, almost five years ago, we'd had a huge fight. I wasn't sure I wanted to go there again, but perhaps she was finally ready to listen. "Maybe you could talk to someone."

My mom threw the flower down on the grass. "This again?" She pushed up off one knee and stood.

I followed, desperate to make her hear me, though I wasn't sure she would. "It might help. A doctor might be able to give you some suggestions on how to move on...give you a new perspective."

Her eyes narrowed. "I don't need a new perspective. I need my husband back! That's what I need!" Her face was red and blotched with anger as she furiously wiped at the new tears streaking her face.

"But he's never coming back," I whispered, barely choking out the words at the stark reality of that sentence.

"You don't think I know that?" she bit out. "Don't you think that is painfully obvious to me every single day?" She beat on her chest with her fist. "Every time something happens and I think about how I wish I could tell your dad about it because he'd think it was funny. Or every morning when I wake up for a split second before reality sets in and I see the empty space where he used to sleep. Every time I see a police car driving around town and I wonder if that was the car he used to drive. Every fiber of my being is more than aware that your dad is gone, Jackie, and a piece of me went with him that I'm never getting back." Her voice broke on her final words.

I gulped hard, my throat constricting at my inability to help take some of her pain away. Saltwater hit my tongue as a tear dripped over my lip. I wasn't even aware I'd been crying. I pulled her into a hug, gripping her tight as grief ripped through the both of us. My throat hurt and my eyes burned by the time we'd gotten ahold of ourselves. Finally, my mom pulled back, but I clung to her upper arms, not wanting to lose contact with her.

She looked me in the eyes—there was so much pain there. "You can't possibly know what it's like. Losing the person that was your other half. It changes you. I hope you never have to find that out."

I swallowed past the painful lump in my throat as an image of Jamie came to my mind. Was I willingly signing up to become my mother years from now and cause my own children the unbearable pain I'd had to deal with?

I was already having difficulty with the intensity of my feelings for Jamie. Fear caused a clammy, cold sweat to break out over my entire body. My legs were weak and shaky and I fought to stay standing.

I'd been kidding myself to think that I was strong enough to face this.

# Chapter Twenty-One

## JAMIE

Frustration had me gripping my steering wheel harder than normal. It had been two days since Jackie had really talked to me. We'd had plans a couple days ago and she'd begged off, saying she wasn't feeling well. Since then she'd been dodging my calls. Something was definitely up with her. Today I knew for certain she wasn't working, so I planned to show up at her place to confront the issue and figure this out. I didn't want to. Jackie had always struck me as someone who, once cornered, would come out swinging. She'd left me no other choice, though. I wasn't going to let her push me away without a fight. Not a chance in hell.

I thought we'd turned a corner the night of the false alarm. It'd been different when we were together that time, and I knew she'd felt it, too. It was intense and moving and, most importantly, there was no way the connection and feelings between us could be denied after that.

I pulled the truck into the driveway, thankful her car was there. Taking a deep breath, I braced myself for what I knew wouldn't be an easy conversation, then exited the truck. I spied her bike leaning against the side of the house before I made my way up the porch steps, which meant she was probably home.

I banged on the door a little louder than intended, my irritation getting the best of me. I heard her feet padding to the door and then silence. My guess was she'd spied me through the peephole.

"I know you're in there, Jackie." Silence again and then I heard her undo the lock and the door swung open.

She looked like shit. Still stunning, but there were bags under her eyes like she hadn't been sleeping, her hair was disheveled, and her skin was paler than normal.

"Are you feeling okay?" I asked. Maybe she really wasn't well.

"Gee, thanks," she clipped back.

I reached out to touch her, and she backed up a step. I ground my teeth together, clenching my jaw. "We need to talk," I said evenly.

"Now isn't a good time, Jamie. Could we do it later?" She heaved out a sigh like I was so exasperating to her.

"No. We're doing it now." I moved past her, into her home. She didn't argue or try to stop me, which I hoped was a good sign. When I reached her living room and turned to face her, I knew it wasn't. Her eyes held a sadness that I hadn't been prepared for. What the hell had happened since I'd seen her last?

"Why are you avoiding me?" I asked.

Her forehead crinkled up in disgust. "I'm not. I told you, I've just—"

I shook my head at her excuses. "Cut the shit, Jackie. Why?" I wasn't going to play this game with her. I believed in being upfront and putting everything out in the open.

She shifted her weight back and forth, and I knew it wasn't going to be good. As a police officer, I was trained to read people's body language, and right now Jackie's was screaming that she'd rather be anywhere but here, having this conversation.

"I don't know what I want." She couldn't even look at me as she toed the hardwood with her bare foot.

"Jackie, look at me." Her gaze swung upward. "What does that mean?" I clutched her shoulders.

"I'm not sure I can see you anymore." She held her breath, staying stock still.

I dropped my hands and tightened them into fists at my side. Drawing a deep breath through my nose, I fought to keep my composure. "Why?" was all I managed through gritted teeth.

"I don't think it's going to work in the long run. Maybe there's no point in prolonging the inevitable." She shrugged, turned away from me, and looked out the window.

No. I wasn't accepting that shitty answer. I reached for her arm and forced her to face me again, but she couldn't even meet my eyes, instead gazing over top of my shoulder.

My mouth fell open. "How could you possibly know that? And after the last time we were together, why would you even entertain the thought?"

She squeezed her eyes shut briefly, like she was in pain. When she opened them, all the brilliant green was gone, replaced with a dull shade more reminiscent of moss. "I don't know what you're talking about."

I dropped my hand from her arm, afraid that in my anger I might hold on harder than I intended. "That's total bullshit. I know I wasn't the only one making love that night. You don't go from that to avoiding me without something happening." I dipped my head looking right into her eyes. "Now. What. Fucking. Happened?" I panted, my breathing labored as I stood there seething and waiting for her to answer me.

She blinked a couple of times, startled by the anger simmering below the surface of my words, or maybe the words themselves. I didn't know and I didn't care. All I cared about was figuring out where her head was really at. Not the half-ass excuses she was feeding me and probably herself, but the truth. The only way I was going to be able to fight for her was if I had some idea what I was fighting against.

"Nothing happened," she said, her voice monotone.

"Jackie!"

She flinched before I saw anger flash in her eyes. It reminded me of the first time we'd met—the firecracker was back. "It was the anniversary of my dad's death, okay? And once again, I had to watch my mom fall apart. Once again, I had to think about all the things my dad has missed since he was killed. Once again, I had to relive it—in my own mind, with my mom...in my dreams. I'm sorry if I'm not all sunshine and rainbows." She wiped a stray tear that had escaped her angry eyes and crossed her arms over her chest.

I rubbed her upper arms and squeezed. "I'm sorry you've had a difficult few days, but what does that have to do with us? You should've told me. I could've been here to support you."

She shook her head, tears springing to her eyes. "No, don't you see? That's the problem. I can't let you do that."

Anger was a hot coal in my stomach. "You can and you will."

"No!" She pulled out of my grip and took a few steps back. "I'm not letting you do this!" she said with a ragged voice.

I frowned, totally confused. "Do what?"

"Worm your way into my life and make me think I can have the fairytale. That everything will be wonderful when it won't. I'll end up like my mom, and I can't do that. I just can't."

"You're being ridiculous." Didn't she realize how I felt about her? Was it not obvious?

"Don't tell me I'm being ridiculous. You have no idea," she said in a haughty tone.

"You're right. I don't. I wish I could understand how you let fear dictate your life." I threw my hands up in the air in front of me. "I've never met someone so afraid of happiness. But the simple fact is that I love you. I love you, Jackie, and I'm not going anywhere."

She blanched and, instead of my confession reassuring her and giving her peace, she continued to fight it. "You can't possibly know that. We haven't been seeing each other that long."

*Fuck.* The girl was impossible to convince. I'd thought we'd gotten past all this. I ran a hand down my face and took a breath, then said with all the sincerity I could, because I wanted her to feel the truth of my words, "I don't need to spend years with you to know that you're the most amazing woman I've ever met. To know that when I'm with you the only thing I feel is pure joy."

Her face crumpled, and she started crying harder. I wanted to go to her and wrap her in my arms—to soothe her and take her pain away—but I fought the urge. Instinct was telling me that she needed to feel this. To work through it and come out the other side on her own and see that she'd survived. See that we were worth fighting for.

"I can't do it." She shook her head frantically. "I can't."

I stepped toward her, and she put her hand out in front of her to keep me back. "Did you hear me? I love you," I said, my voice almost pleading and cracking on my declaration of love for her.

"Which is why I have to let you go," she cried. "I'm not strong enough for this. I'm not brave enough."

I blinked at her, stared at her, dumbfounded. I was numb as the agony of what she was doing started to set in. My breaths were heavy, and my heart pounded away in my chest. "I'm not going to let you do this."

She wiped at the tears running down her face. "You don't have a choice. I can't be with you, Jamie. Go find someone less screwed up than I am." She sucked in an uneven breath and her lips trembled.

Every muscle in my body was so tense I started to ache. How could she be doing this? I'd thought when she realized the depth of my feelings for her, and vice versa, that she'd come around and see a future for us. Instead those feelings had sent her running.

"You're really willing to throw away what we have because you're scared of what could maybe happen in the future?" My voice broke at the end of my sentence.

She hugged her arms around herself and nodded. "I have no choice," she whispered back.

"There's always a choice." I leaned in and pointed at her. "You're just too fucking stubborn and scared to see it."

"Go," she sobbed. "Please just go."

I let out a growl of frustration, balling my hands into fists at my sides. Then I stomped toward the front door, pausing when I reached her side. "Whether you realize it or not, this is a self-fulfilling prophecy. One day you'll see that and regret this."

She didn't respond, didn't even turn her head to look at me.

I continued on out of her house, out of her life, and completely out of my fucking mind that she'd pushed me away knowing how we both felt about one another.

It was far from over, though. I was determined that this was only a chapter in what would be a long story between the two of us. Jackie may think the entire book had been written, read, and shut tight never to be looked at again. Over my dead body.

ELISABETH GRACE

# Chapter Twenty-Two

## Jackie

I lay in my darkened room with the windows closed, blinds down, and curtains drawn. I was on nights this week, and it was the third day in a row I'd spent the afternoon in bed, wallowing before I had to get ready for work. Even though I felt it was best in the long run, I was having trouble getting Jamie's pained expression out of my mind. That and the anger he'd felt for me before leaving were occupying the majority of my thoughts these past few days. I had to remind myself, more than a few times, that this was what I wanted.

And tonight promised to be worse because he was also working and there was a good chance I would have to hear his deep voice on the line and possibly speak to him directly if I had to send him on some calls.

I missed him. More than I even anticipated.

I missed having him near, hearing his voice, being intimate. Even though it was still summer, the past few days had felt like a pale landscape, like all the color had seeped out of my life.

I glanced lifelessly over at the clock on my nightstand. I had to get in the shower now if I was going to be on time for work. It was going to be a long night...

About halfway through my shift, I got a call from someone reporting a burglary in progress. I had managed not to radio Jamie thus far, but the call was in his section so it appeared my luck had run out.

Taking a deep breath, I braced myself for my first contact with him since I'd pushed him away. I had no doubt he'd keep it professional, but still.

After sighing, I called for his car. "Ninety-nine, a four-fifty-nine."

He answered right away. "Ninety-nine, go ahead."

I closed my eyes at the sound of his voice and then continued. "One-seventy-six Main Street, David's Jewelers, passerby reports seeing someone in the store."

"Ninety-nine, copy."

"Ninety-nine, ten-oh. The RP says they may have seen a gun in the waistband of the subject."

Now that I'd gotten past our first contact, my body tensed as I focused on the dangerous situation he'd be walking into. I called the other car out, though it would take that officer longer to arrive. This was the part I hated. After I sent any of the first responders out on a dangerous call, the waiting was the worst.

I shifted in my seat and tapped my foot on the floor, trying to release some of the tension that had my chest and throat in a chokehold. God, I'd been stupid to think that by pushing Jamie away I'd been sparing myself the torture of worrying about him. It was too late—he'd already become too important for me to simply cast aside my feelings.

When Jamie's voice came back over the line, my tension increased tenfold. "Ninety-nine, ten-ninety-seven."

He'd arrived on the scene.

"Ninety-nine, check," I said, following protocol, though I felt like doing anything but. My breathing was shallow as I waited for some kind of report back.

"Seventy-six, ten-ninety-seven," the other officer said.

I released a small breath, relieved to know Jamie now had back up with him. I pushed my pen over and over again into my thigh, to the point that it became painful, but I was happy for the small distraction from my wayward thoughts as I tried to picture what could be happening at the jewelry store. Was the perp still there or long gone by now?

"Eleven-ninety-nine." The voice and the code over the line had my heart seize in my chest, and I sat frozen in my seat, my blood running cold. That was the code for an officer in trouble...and it hadn't been Jamie's voice.

I let out the breath I'd been holding and came back to myself, starting the Code thirty-three tone. "Eleven-ninety-nine. Officer needs help, all units respond Code three. One-seven-six Main Street, David's Jewelers."

"Seventy-nine, I need an ambulance, officer down! I repeat, officer down!" the officer assisting Jamie yelled. "Suspect took off on foot, south on Main Street. White male, late twenties, black T-shirt and jeans, black ball cap."

"Seventy-nine, check," I said, fighting back tears, my hands shaking. I was trying to keep my head in the game, I really was, but visions of Jamie lying bloody on the sidewalk pushed into my head. I squeezed my eyes shut, trying desperately to dislodge them.

Once I'd made all the calls and the ambulance was close to the scene, I pushed away from my desk and called my supervisor over. I was shaking and nauseous as I explained the situation and asked if he could call someone else in to cover the rest of my shift. I was desperate to get to Jamie. He had to know how I felt—that if I could change things I'd never have pushed him away...he was *everything* to me. I could only hope that he'd still be alive by the time I got there.

# Chapter Twenty-Three

## Jackie

I ran into the waiting area of the emergency room and it was complete chaos—full of uniformed and off duty officers from all ranks.

For a moment, I searched for Don. He would have gotten a call, even though he'd recently retired. I spotted him in the far corner of the room. When he caught my gaze, he said something to the person he was talking to then made his way over to me, his expression anguished, displaying exactly how I felt inside.

I couldn't move. I was rooted to the floor, afraid to reach him in case he had bad news. When he finally reached me, he immediately hugged me to him, rubbing his hand up and down my back. The tears I'd managed to hold in the entire ride came bursting out, overflowing down my face.

"It's gonna be okay, honey," he soothed. "Shh."

"Is he...is he?" I couldn't get the words out, couldn't form them on my tongue.

"No, honey. He should be fine," he said in a soothing way. "He was shot in the vest and the arm, but that injury looks to be more of a graze."

"Oh, thank God." Relief rushed through me so fast my knees were buckling. Don had to hold me tighter to keep me standing.

"Come on. Come sit down." He led me over to an unoccupied seat and helped me  sit. I hunched over, pressing my hands to my face and rocking back and forth. I was so thankful to hear that Jamie's injuries weren't worse, but the full weight of how easily it could've been a different outcome was hitting me.

Don continued to soothe me until I recovered enough to sit up and speak. "I was working when the call came in. I didn't know what happened. I heard the officer down code and rushed straight here."

Don pursed his lips and frowned, while I rubbed at the tear tracks with the sleeve of my shirt. "What's going on? This is more than being upset that a colleague was in danger." He went quiet for a moment, then said, "I heard some murmurings that something might be going on between you two. Is that the case?"

I bit my lip and nodded. "It was, but I messed it all up and pushed him away because I was scared."

Don searched my face. "Of what?"

I heaved out a sigh. "That I'd end up like my mother. Brokenhearted and alone, pining away for a ghost for the rest of my life."

Don nodded thoughtfully, then brought me in for another hug. "Oh, sweetie. I'll be the first to tell you that being a cop is a dangerous job. Things can go wrong in a second, and every day you put that uniform on and head in for a shift you have no idea what's going to go down. Tonight is a perfect example. But when it's our time, it's our time." He pulled away and held me by the shoulders. "I could walk out of here and drop dead of a heart attack, or get hit by a car crossing the street. The fact that I'm a cop doesn't mean I'm destined to die on the job."

He was right. Of course he was. I nodded, pressing my lips together for a moment to prevent more tears from falling. "I know what you're saying makes sense. And I was doing good until I saw my mom last week. She was a complete mess like she is every year and it brought it all back. I panicked." I frowned, remembering how stupid I'd been.

Don gave me a small smile. "Look, I only got to work with Jamie for a short time, but one thing I can tell you about him is that he's fair and reasonable. If you explain to him the error of your ways, I'm sure he'll come around."

I brushed the sticky tears off my face and wrapped myself in my arms. God, I hoped he was right. If Jamie refused to forgive me and give me another chance I wasn't sure what I'd do.

Sometime later the doctor came out to give an update to the crowd of officers waiting. It was just as Don had said. Jamie would have some bruised ribs and he'd have to watch the wound in his arm to be sure it didn't get infected, but beyond that he should make a full recovery.

The doctor wanted to keep him overnight for observation and said Jamie could have a few visitors that night before resting, though we could only go in two at a time.

Apparently, my waterworks had secured me a front-of-the-line pass because everyone urged me to go first. So it was with trepidation and an extreme amount of hesitance that I made my way down the hall to the room Jamie was in. I was thankful everyone had insisted I go in alone since I wasn't sure what kind of reception to expect from him. Nerves were wracking my body, leaving my muscles feeling weak.

I knocked softly on the closed door.

"Come in," I heard Jamie say.

I pushed the door open so he could see it was me, then I stood in the doorway, waiting for his reaction.

He looked at me with tired eyes and heaved out a heavy sigh. "What're you doing here?" he asked in what sounded like a pained voice. He leaned back into his pillow to stare at the ceiling. "Shouldn't you be working still?"

"I left," was all I managed to say.

"Obviously. Why?" he asked.

Here came the hard part. Taking a deep breath, I closed the door behind me and made my way over to the end of his bed. My hands were in front of me, fidgeting, making my nerves obvious. "I came because...because I realized I made a mistake. I shouldn't have pushed you away. I might've tried to kick you out of my life, but I've realized that doesn't mean you're out of my heart. When I knew you were in trouble—" My sentence broke off as I started sobbing again, the helpless feeling I'd had when I'd gotten his distress call once again overwhelming me.

"Oh, Jackie..." Jamie reached a hand out to me. I couldn't help noticing it was the arm without the bandage.

I didn't hesitate, moving around the bed to clutch it with my own. "I'm sorry, Jamie. I'm sorry I pushed you away because I was so scared. I panicked. Last week was the anniversary of my dad's death. Seeing my mom so messed up after all these years and listening to her go on and on about how happy she was one minute and then the next...it messed with my head and reminded me of my feelings for you. I couldn't deal. I'm so sorry."

More tears leaked from my eyes that felt raw from all the salt water they'd already seen tonight. I reached for a tissue on the bedside table and wiped under my nose then finally sat down on the chair beside the bed, leaning my head against the mattress. Jamie's hand came down and stroked my hair while I let it all out. I was determined that this would be the last time I allowed fear like this to rule my life.

As my wracking sobs began to slow, I realized that Jamie still hadn't really said anything. I needed to know how he felt and whether I still had a chance with him. I brought my head up to look at him. Even with everything he'd been through tonight, he was still such a beautiful, masculine man.

"Can you forgive me?" I whispered.

He closed his eyes briefly. "How do I know you're not going to do it again? It was painful for me, too."

"Because I love you. I love you and I never want to let you go. Whether we have two years or twenty together, I never want to be apart from you again. You've already made me a prisoner to my heart and the simple fact is that, unless I'm with you, I'm going to be unhappy. I'm willing to risk what the future may bring if it means I can spend the present with you."

He said nothing for a moment, just stared at me with an unreadable expression. When he finally let out a breath, a slow smile crept across his face and he opened his arms up to me. "Finally. I feel like I've been waiting forever and a day to hear those words from you. I do forgive you. All I want is to be with you, too."

I'd braced myself to hear the worst from him and it took a moment for his response to sink in. When it did I sprung up from my seat, tears of joy now streaking down my face, and leaned forward to kiss him. But before I could lean in all the way, Jamie grasped my face, stopping my progress.

"You have to promise me one thing," he said.

I nodded frantically. I'd promise him anything if it meant we could move forward.

"Next time you're feeling even the least bit panicked

or unsure you have to tell me." He dipped his head, pinning me with an intense glare. "Don't pull that shit again."

I smiled at him, relief coursing through my body. "I can do that. Promise."

"Good." He grinned. "Now bring those lips here. I've missed them."

I leaned down the rest of the way and brought my lips to his. The usual heat inside of me began to build as his tongue brushed against mine. He brought his hand to the back of my head and increased the tempo. I leaned forward a little more until I heard Jamie suck in a breath. Pulling back quickly, I saw that he was wincing and pressing on one of his ribs.

I jerked back, afraid that I was hurting him. "Are you okay?"

He nodded. "Yeah, looks like you're going to have to go easy on me for a bit."

"No make-up sex, I suppose." I fake pouted.

Jamie's eyes narrowed. "There will absolutely, one hundred percent, positively be some make-up sex when I get out of here. No matter how painful."

I chuckled and cupped his cheek. "I think we'll have to clear that with your doctor," I said in a sing-song voice.

"Jackie," Jamie warned.

I giggled. "Relax, big guy. We've got all the time in the world."

He reached for my hand and, when he took it, he squeezed it and smiled. Love poured out of his eyes and I knew he saw the same emotion in my own reflected back at him. "Yes, I suppose we do."

For the first time ever, I found myself really believing it.

# *Epilogue*
## *One Year Later...*

## *Jackie*

I drove my car down the country back roads, singing along to *The Civil Wars* and wishing for the thousandth time that they hadn't broken up. The warm summer air was blowing in through the car's open windows, tugging loose some of the hair in my ponytail. I inhaled a deep breath. Only the odd house dotted the landscape, but someone nearby had recently cut their grass, the smell of which always reminded me of the lazy summer days from my youth when I used to play on the front lawn while my dad cut our yard. That was so long ago.

I was reflecting on how much had changed in the past year when I realized I was only about a mile from where Jamie and I had first met. Since admitting my love for him, I'd slowly been able to resist the fear that had once had such a vice grip on me and ruled over all the decisions in my life. I still worried for him when he was on shift, but I'd learned not to borrow trouble—why stress over something that hasn't and may never happen? They say you become what you think about most and, in trying so hard not to turn out like my mother, I had become exactly like her—alone and afraid.

Not anymore. The past year with Jamie had brought me more happiness than one girl deserved in a lifetime. I didn't miss my party girl lifestyle. I still had fun—he'd never tame me entirely—but gone were the random hookups and crazy parties, and in their place was the safety and security of knowing I was truly loved for who I was.

In seeing how happy I was with Jamie, my mom had finally agreed to talk to someone. She was doing a little better, but it was baby steps. Sadly, Jamie's dad's Alzheimer's had continued to get worse and he'd developed dementia as well. Denny now lived in a nursing home where someone was able to keep an eye on him twenty-four-seven.

As I came around the last curve before I'd pass the spot of our first meeting, I noticed a police car parked on the side of the road ahead. I glanced down to my speedometer to make sure I wasn't speeding. The last thing I needed was *another* ticket in the exact same spot.

I slowed the car down as I approached and the driver's side door opened. My stomach did a weird flip when I saw Jamie get out of the car. What was he doing here? Hitting my brakes, I pulled my car over onto the dirt shoulder and came to a stop behind him. I turned the car off and got out with a big smile on my face.

"Fancy seeing you here," I said with a grin.

Jamie walked toward me, looking as sexy as ever in his black police uniform. He was smiling but didn't say a word. Although the look in his eyes told me something was going on. His expression was one of adoration and joy, but I sensed an underlying nervousness.

*Why?*

As he came to stand in front of me, I asked, "What's going on?" I searched his face for answers.

Jamie took a deep breath, and I swear I saw a glimmer of moisture in the corner of his eyes. He took my face in his hands and tenderly cupped my cheeks, brushing my skin with his thumbs. "Jackie, you know how much I love you."

I nodded, wondering where this was going.

"A year ago we met in this exact spot. This is where my life really began. This is where I found my purpose. I had a million ideas of how I wanted to do this and what would make it special. I wanted you to have a story you could tell our children someday, but my mind kept coming back to where it all started."

All the breath pushed out of my lungs as I realized where he was going with this.

"I never told you this, but the moment I met you I knew you were something special." Sincerity shone in his expression and rang through in his tone. "I didn't dare to think you could ever truly be mine, but you were under my skin in seconds. As I came to realize what a strong, independent, and sensual woman you are, I knew I had to make you mine. Our first meeting was rocky...started out rough. That's exactly why I had to do this here. When I ask you my next question I want you to remember that even though there will be times that aren't easy, if we're open and honest with each other, we can get through anything."

Suddenly, Jamie dropped down on one knee and reached into his pocket. I gasped and put my hand to my mouth.

"Will you bring even more joy to my life by being my wife?" He opened a black jewelry case, his hands shaking slightly, his expression hopeful. Nestled inside was an oval-shaped diamond surrounded by smaller diamonds.

It sparkled, the sunlight glittering and reflecting off its multi-faceted surface.

I was overcome and unable to speak for a moment as all my emotions seemed to lodge in my throat. But as I gazed down at his face, I knew that his was the face I wanted to look at forever. I wanted to see the color wash out of it during the long north eastern winters. I wanted to see his eyes tear up as he gazed down upon a child of ours for the first time. I wanted to see the lines and creases that would be etched into his skin decades from now. My heart swelled and felt too big for my chest because I wanted everything with this man.

Finally, as a single tear slid down my cheek, I was able to pull it together. "Yes, yes!" I cried, pulling on his hand so he would stand up.

He let out a relieved breath and rose and I wrapped my arms around his waist in a fierce hug, nestling my face in his neck and giving him one chaste kiss after another. I pulled back, laughing and crying at the same time. Jamie's grin was so wide it could have split his face in two. He was laughing as he took the ring from the box. I held out my left hand for him, and he slid the ring on. It looked even more beautiful on my hand because he was the one who had picked it and placed it there.

"I love you so much!" I wrapped my arms around his neck, and Jamie lifted me by the waist and swung me around.

"I was afraid you were going to say no when you took so long." He set me down, but I didn't remove my arms from around him.

"Not on your life, mister. You're stuck with me now."

Jamie laughed then leaned in and placed a soft kiss on my lips, looking deep into my eyes, into my soul. "There's no place I'd rather be."

*That's right, Officer.*

I sighed and leaned into his chest. Standing there listening to his heartbeat, I couldn't have been more thankful that this man had come into my life and helped me learn how to trust enough to let my own heart beat for someone else again.

## The End

# *About The Author*

One of the best ways to support an author is by leaving a review! If you enjoyed Jackie and Jamie's story I'd appreciate it if you'd consider leaving a review, whether short or long, on the retailer's site where you purchased the book.

Elisabeth has a soft spot for happily ever-afters and a hot spot for alpha males. If she's not curled up somewhere with a romance novel in one hand and chocolate in the other you can probably find her typing madly on her keyboard creating her next story. She currently lives outside Toronto, Canada with her husband, two small children, and a killer cat.

### Questions? Comments?

I love to hear from readers! Feel free to connect with me via e-mail at authorelisabethgrace@gmail.com or through social media. You can find all the links on my website at Elisabeth-Grace.com. Want to know when my next book comes out? Sign up for my newsletter via my website!!

I take your privacy seriously. I will not sell your e-mail address. I will only contact you with important news like cover reveals, special giveaways for newsletter subscribers, and to tell you when a new book is available. I won't be spamming your inbox every week.

# *Other Books By*
# *Elisabeth Grace*

**The Limelight Series**
Rumor Has It (Limelight #1)
Picture Perfect (Limelight #2)
Collateral Agreement (Limelight #3)

**Maine Attraction Series**
Indecision
Indiscretion (Keep reading for a sneak peek!)

# *Acknowledgements*

Like this novel, I'm going to try to keep this one short and sweet! ;)

This book originally appeared in Brenda Novak's Sweet Seduction Box Set in order to help raise money for Diabetes research and education. So I have to thank her for asking me to be a part of such an important project. I'm not sure this book would have ever been written if not for her invitation.

To both my editors, Angela and Megan. Thank you as always for your efforts in helping to turn this book into the best story that it could be. Your support, professionalism and (sometimes) cheerleading will not be forgotten.

Writing can be a very isolating job. You sit at your computer night after night by yourself with only your thoughts to turn to. I've been lucky to find some amazing readers, bloggers, and authors within the reading community. These connections that I've made are near and dear to my heart and are the best part of this writing gig!

Last but never least, to my family who supports me and allow me the luxury of going after my dreams, even when it means my head is in the clouds most of the time...I love you all more than you'll ever comprehend.

# *Indiscretion Vol 1-4*

Fuck and chuck. Pump and dump. Hit it and quit it. One night stand. Didn't matter how I branded it—that's all she had wanted it to be. That much was clear when she left me with my pants down and my dick still out.

What she hadn't counted on was fate intervening and our worlds colliding—again.

The day I showed back up in the life of Chloe Griffins, I knew I had to have her again. My body was hungry for another taste. Like an addict, I'd been craving another hit for months, and there she was—flesh and bone, tits and ass.

The fact that she worked for the competition should've been reason enough for me to leave her alone. I had a job to do that summer and fucking Chloe wasn't part of it. But I was like a man possessed.

I'd do whatever it took to have her again.

# *Chapter One*

## *Chloe*

"If you don't find a man soon, you're going to die a born-again virgin."

I directed an exasperated sigh at my best friend Jackie. "Well, it's a good thing I'm feeling adventurous then. Maybe we should find someone for me to flirt with tonight."

I set my half-empty martini down on the expensive chrome-and-glass VIP table I'd been able to secure at On The Rocks, New York City's newest high-end celebrity hangout. Tonight we were here to celebrate Jackie's upcoming nuptials. Glancing around, I took in the carrera marble floors, black fabric-draped walls, and large circular banquettes running along the perimeter of the room. I was a long way from small-town Bar Harbor, Maine.

Jackie rubbed her hands together in obvious anticipation. "Ooooh, I like the sound of this. Let's pick one. Or should we wait for the rest of the girls to stop flirting with the bartender and get back here with the drinks?" I glanced over to the bar and sure enough the rest of the bridal party was there laughing it up with one of the workers. Before I could say anything, Jackie pointed across the room. "What about that guy over there?"

I looked across the dim bar to the wine-colored, velvet banquettes, where an attractive man sat pondering the wine list. "You know I'm not into blonds. Two blonds together, can you imagine? How would we ever figure out what body parts go where?" I batted my eyes feigning innocence.

Jackie chuckled at my lame attempt at a joke, while I continued my inspection of our fellow patrons. Not much to choose from, which was disappointing. On the one night I'd decided to let loose a little, there wasn't anyone worth letting loose with. I certainly wasn't interested in the middle-aged man with the small paunch and a wedding ring, trolling for women at the bar. Or the work-obsessed Wall Street type with the suspenders over his dress shirt who didn't seem to be letting his friends get a word in edgewise. And the artsy guy was too outside the box. His bright red jeans, painted on his ass, looked like they'd been dragged behind a bus. But this was New York City—they probably cost a small fortune.

I scrunched my face up in distaste then turned in the other direction and locked gazes with a set of piercing blue eyes. The wall sconces and the lighted glass behind the bar offered the only illumination in the room, but it didn't matter. I could see from here—this guy was smokin'. And not like a 'let's cook some marshmallows over the fire' kind of smokin'. He was three-alarm blaze, call-in-the-water-bombers smokin'.

I swallowed, my lips parting while my eyes took in his wholly male presence. He was standing beside a table, and his tailored grey suit hugged his body—a body that sure as hell had spent a lot of time at the gym. His dark hair had a slight wave to it and brushed the top of his back collar.

I held his gaze for a long moment as the rest of the people milling about the room seemed to fade away. The reality that I was blatantly staring at the stranger floated into my consciousness, and I cleared my throat as I diverted my gaze. But not before seeing his sexy, lopsided grin, complete with dimple and a perfect set of pearly whites.

Heat rose up my neck, and I traced the condensation pattern of a cup no longer there.

"Wow. He's something else."

I turned my attention back to my friend and gave her a weak smile. "He sure is."

With a suspicious smile, Jackie said, "I haven't seen this side of you in a while. I have to say, I like it."

I rolled my eyes. "I'm not that bad, am I?"

"Well, not at my bachelorette party, you're not," she said, sliding a shot in front of me. "I still can't believe you got us in this place."

It hadn't been easy. The group of us were only in town for the weekend, but luckily one of my past clients had a connection with the owner, who'd agreed to let us use the table without the usual bottle service requirement. Five hundred a bottle was too rich for my blood—and my bank account. In exchange for the table, I'd committed the ultimate sin and agreed to sell his oceanfront home at a reduced commission when the time came. Tit for tat, that was always the way. But a maid of honor couldn't put a price on keeping her nearest and dearest friend happy, now could she?

"Bottoms up," Jackie said, picking her shot up off the table.

I fidgeted in my seat, pulling down the too-short hem of my dress. How I'd let Jackie talk me into wearing

177

this thing I'd never know. "I think I've had enough for now," I said and looked over at my friend.

"Come on," Jackie whined and placed the shot back on the table. "You've finally let loose. It's my bachelorette party...please?"

"Don't bat those eyes at me."

Jackie continued to give me her best version of a puppy-dog face, which in her inebriated state more closely resembled a botched Botox job.

I laughed. "You were always the noceur not me."

She rolled her eyes. "Alright word nerd, none of that tonight. I plan to have *way* too many drinks in me to try and figure out what the hell you're saying."

I shook my head and gave her a cheeky grin, knowing I'd used the word purposely just to bait her. I'd had a thing for words as long as I could remember. I loved discovering rarely used words, but my absolute favorite was finding words in other languages that had no English equivalent.

Jackie didn't share my love for all things literary. But it *was* just like my free-spirited friend to want to crank the party up a notch. We'd met twenty-eight years earlier when we were babies and both our moms had sent us to the same babysitter. I couldn't remember a time in our lives when we hadn't been there for each other.

"Fine, pass it over." I reached for the shot, sure it would be my undoing. "But I can't be held responsible for my actions." I laughed. Jackie always did have a way of talking me into things.

I sprinkled some salt on my wrist, licked it off, and tossed back the tequila. Grimacing, I grabbed a lime off the table, put it in my mouth, and sucked. The tequila burned my throat all the way down to my stomach. It was awful stuff, but a welcome distraction from the feeling of loneliness that seemed to have taken permanent residence inside me.

The idea of Jackie settling down still seemed so strange to me. "How is it that after all the sleeping around you did, you ended up being the one to find Prince Charming?" I asked.

Jackie laughed. "I keep telling you, Chloe, all work and no play won't make you happy. And it definitely won't get you laid." Her face turned serious and she bumped my shoulder with her own. "Come on, what gives? You haven't seemed yourself the past few weeks. It's almost been radio silence unless I call you. I love that you're having fun tonight, but I can tell something's been on your mind. Is it because you haven't been out with anyone in a while?"

I looked across the room and saw the rest of the girls were now sidled up to some guy at the bar who looked to be buying them a round of drinks. "God, no," I muttered. "I haven't been out with anyone because there's no one worth going out with. We can't all be as lucky as you and have Prince Charming rescue us from the side of the road when we get a flat tire."

Jackie's eyes narrowed. "And you don't stand a chance of meeting Prince Charming unless he up and falls on your windshield while you're driving around town showing houses," Jackie countered. "I think you deliberately avoid situations where you might meet him."

"I don't need to meet Prince Charming...I'm perfectly fine with the way my life is now." The conviction in my voice almost made me believe it myself—almost. Attempting to lighten the mood, I added, "Maybe I'll become a nun, be celibate, and live happily ever after."

Jackie flicked her long, black hair off her shoulder and pressed her lips together, her green eyes unblinking as she stared impatiently at me. "Sounds like a lot of fun," she said dryly. "Can I make a suggestion? Try having fun for the time being. Find some hot guy, have lots of hot sex, and don't worry about whether he checks all the boxes on your extensive list of items meant to weed out any man with a pulse. Seriously, what's the worst that could happen?"

I twisted my lips to the side and pretended to think about it. "Hmm...I fall madly in love with said hot guy, not be able to live without him, and turn into Glenn Close's character in Fatal Attraction?" I laughed.

"Okay, smartass. Ever the optimist," Jackie quipped, sarcasm evident in her voice. "We all have needs. And you haven't gotten laid in forever. Hellooo—it's called sexual frustration."

I could always trust Jackie to put it all out there without softening the edges. "I'm not sexually frustrated. They make stuff to take care of that sort of thing," I teased.

"It's not the same and you know it. A vibrator isn't going to kiss you like it can't get enough. You can't feel the heat of its skin against you or gaze into its eyes when it's on top of you, just before it—"

I raised my hand up to stop her from continuing. "Okay, I get your point."

I had that familiar pang in my chest, a lonely ache coupled with another ache brewing further down as I imagined what it would be like to be with a man again. Having that intimacy with someone would be nice, but some things just weren't worth taking the risk for. Life had thrown a lot at me, and I'd learned that being that dependent on another person for my happiness wasn't worth the pain left behind in their absence. My sister was all I had left now.

"I understand." Jackie looked at me sadly. "After what happened with Jeff, I get it. But that was forever ago. Maybe you could keep it casual? You're gorgeous. You've never had a shortage of male attention."

I sighed. I was no fool. I knew exactly what Jackie's end game was. She hoped that if I put myself out there, I'd magically stumble into Mr. Right like she had. *Never. Going. To. Happen.* I just wasn't that girl who had everything fall into place for her. My past was proof enough.

Jackie's hand came down on top of mine. "I want you to be happy. I worry about you. What are you going to do once your sister's moved halfway across the country? I'm concerned about where that's going to leave you. Ever since Jeff, you've kept every guy at arm's length. And that was years ago. You need a man in your life."

I gulped. Jackie's concern was genuine, and none of what she'd said was news to me. I'd had those same thoughts plenty of times, but I kept pushing them away, telling myself I'd deal with them later. Well, later was fast approaching.

Hearing it from Jackie's mouth brought home the realization that I couldn't continue to put off dealing with the inevitable—my sister was leaving for college. Dread formed in the pit of my stomach as I tried to picture how I'd fill my days once she was gone. The person who had been my primary focus for the past ten years would soon no longer be a part of my daily routine. I'd taken a chance on Jeff and after how that turned out, well, I'd thought it was better to focus on raising my sister and securing my own future. My love life could wait.

"If you'd walked in on your boyfriend banging his secretary on his desk, you wouldn't be keen on dating either," I deadpanned. "But that's not it...I've been stressed out with work. I'm not sure I'm going to meet my sales quota by the deadline. I need that bonus," I said, massaging my temple. Impending loneliness had been the least of my concerns over the past few weeks. Ever since my Broker's offer to buy into the firm, I'd been working like mad to make every sale I could at the new condo building.

"Sales aren't going well?" Jackie asked.

"Well enough." I shrugged. "Still, I'd feel better if I'd reached my goal already, or if I was only a handful of sales away. That's the only way I'm ever going to have enough money to buy into the brokerage."

Months ago, the broker in my office approached me with the deal of a lifetime. To semi-retire, he was going to need a partner to keep the brokerage afloat on a day-to-day basis. He'd offered me first dibs on the buy-in, saying he'd always admired my 'grit and determination.' I was ecstatic, of course. I needed this. I had no college education to fall back on, and years ago I'd grown tired of chasing the next deal.

God, if I could make this happen, it would change my life. It would mean that even after losing my mother so young, I'd have the stability and security I'd always sought.

"You're a great agent," Jackie assured me with an encouraging smile. "I'm sure it'll all come together."

I returned the smile though I didn't really feel it. "Thanks, but you're my best friend. You have to say that." I let out a heavy sigh, wishing I shared my friend's confidence, and pushed the feeling down. Now was not the time to reflect on life. I was here to have a good time and celebrate Jackie's happiness—to hell with my own issues. Tonight was all about my best friend, and I'd be damned if my own problems were going to bring my friend down. Jackie loved a good time, and as maid of honor it was my job to make sure I delivered.

"Enough talk about the heavy stuff. Let's get back to finding a guy for me to flirt with tonight."

"I thought we'd already found one." She nodded mischievously toward the insanely hot guy with the blue eyes.

"Yeah, right," I scoffed. "A little out of my league, I think."

"Oh, please," Jackie frowned. "For all we know, he could be covered in back hair and have a small dick."

I burst out laughing and gave my friend a light smack across the arm. It took me a minute to catch my breath. "You're horrible." I grinned at her. "Do you know how long it's been since I flirted with someone? Maybe I should start with more of an average Joe."

I was in the mood for some innocent fun tonight. Being away from home and all the memories and responsibilities it held seemed to have had that affect. Even so, I had a feeling any conversation with the blue-eyed stranger had the potential to turn into something not entirely innocent.

"Alright then." Jackie leaned in to give me a hug as the rest of the bridal party returned from the bar and placed down a variety of drinks and shots. In the spirit of the evening, I picked up a shot of God-knows-what neon concoction and held it in the air. The other girls followed suit.

Smiling at my friend, I shoved down the lump of nostalgia. "I'd like to propose a toast to Jackie and her upcoming nuptials. May she and Jamie have a long and happy life together, full of nothing but love, trust, joy…and because it's Jackie, a whole lot of mind-blowing sex."

All the girls cheered and clinked the assortment of drinks and shots before tossing them back. Jackie beamed. Whether a result of alcohol, love, or the fact that I was looking to have a little fun, I couldn't be sure. I hoped it wasn't the latter or my friend would end up disappointed. Despite what I'd said, I had no intention of pursuing anything beyond a mild flirtation with anyone—blue-eyed stranger included.

Ninety minutes, one drink, and two shots later, I stood in front of the gilded bathroom mirror, mulling over my earlier conversation with Jackie.

It was hard to admit she was right, but I knew it wasn't normal for a twenty-eight-year-old single female to put as much effort into avoiding a relationship as most others put into finding one. Even so, I wasn't interested in opening up my heart to be hurt again. My father, my mother, and my ex—all gone. My sister would be added to that list soon. All for different reasons, but gone just the same.

I had no illusions of a happily-ever-after for myself, but there was no denying that a little sexual satisfaction would be a welcome addition to my life. I'd never considered casual sex before, but I hadn't thought I'd be alone at this age either.

I smoothed the material down on the front of my dress. *Focus, Chloe.* No more thoughts about sex.

But my mind kept wandering.

Maybe if the sex came with no strings attached...and with someone who looked like that guy I'd noticed earlier in the bar. Spending a night between the sheets with a guy like that certainly wouldn't be a hardship.

Shit, I'd lasted all of five seconds not thinking about sex. I had the mind of a thirteen-year-old boy tonight. Had to be the booze talking—I sounded nothing like myself.

*Whatever.* It wasn't like I had to make a decision on the spot. For tonight, I'd have fun at my bestie's bachelorette party and see how I felt in the morning—after the effects of the alcohol wore off.

My arms were heavy as I fished a small comb out of my purse and ran it through my long blonde strands. Some hairspray would be good, but there was no sign of the usual assortment of beauty products on the expansive granite counter. Too bad, especially since there hadn't been enough room to fit any in the microscopic cocktail bag I was carrying.

I returned the comb to my purse and straightened the pale yellow dress Jackie had talked me into wearing. Apparently hems that reached only mid-thigh were for streetwalkers and the trendy alike. As satisfied as I was going to get, I headed toward the bathroom door to re-join the girls. My legs felt leaden, like I'd spent hours in a hot tub, as my stilettos clicked on the marble floor.

With my hand on the door, I glanced back to make sure I hadn't left anything on the counter when I noticed...urinals?

What. The. Hell.

Shit. *Say it isn't so.* No, no. I did not go into the men's room. No freaking way. But with one more panicked glance, I realized I most definitely *did. Definitely blaming this one on the booze.* Either that or the artsy signage outside the door that left anyone guessing as to whether the figure resembled a man or a woman.

Turning quickly to make my escape, I whirled around and took a step forward, only to run straight into the opening bathroom door. Pain exploded in my nose and tears immediately pricked my eyes. Someone was entering the bathroom and pushing in the door.

Stunned, I took a step backward and shook my head. Warm hands settled on my upper arms and steadied me. I looked up and was speechless. The hands belonged to the man with the memorable blue eyes I'd spotted earlier. *Of course, why go for slight mortification when you could really out-do yourself?*

Sex on legs—that was my only coherent thought at that moment. And I was pretty sure from the grin on his face and the seduction in his eyes that I'd made his hit list.

# *Chapter Two*

## *Chloe*

"I'm so sorry, are you okay?" Sex on legs said.

I didn't respond. Just stood there, taking in the fine specimen of a man—gaping at him with a dropped jaw. I'm surprised there wasn't drool making its way down my chin. Dark stubble covering chiseled features led down to an even more defined body. The black shirt under his suit jacket stretched across his muscular frame. It was open at the collar, highlighting his golden skin. I wondered if the expanse of his muscled chest had that same golden glow. The suit looked expensive, certainly custom-made. There was no way he'd pulled it off a sales rack at J.C. Penney. It fit too well. He smelled of expensive cologne mixed with expensive cognac.

I blinked a few times and came back to myself. God, how long had I been standing here, gaping at him like an idiot?

"I'm fine." It was mostly true. My nose was tender

but it wasn't anything I couldn't handle. I moved to get free of his grip. It wasn't that I didn't like the feel of his large hands. I liked it *too* much. What I really wanted to do was close my eyes and memorize the sensation of his hands on my bare skin.

"I've had women fall all over me before, but this is taking it to a new level," he said with a hint of amusement.

I gave a small smirk, hoping I indicated that I didn't find his remark humorous.

He took me in slowly from head to toe. "I'm pretty sure I'm in the right place...but there's certainly nothing masculine about you."

I felt his gaze travel up my body. My skin heated under his close examination of what I was now certain was a dress with too little material. My face burned red hot, and I pulled at the hem of my skirt. "My mistake—obviously."

A slow grin spread across his face, showcasing a killer smile. "Well, it looks like your mistake is my good fortune. I was hoping to connect with you at some point this evening. You've saved me the discomfort of approaching a table full of women."

"You were? I mean, you saw me out there?" I motioned with my hand to the main room.

"You're a difficult woman not to notice."

"Oh." If bumping into the door with my face hadn't been sobering, this statement certainly was. My eyes widened in surprise. I wouldn't have thought a man like him would look twice at me.

He laughed, probably because I was still stupidly standing inside the men's restroom having a conversation with him. *Smooth, Chloe.*

"Give me a minute and we'll continue this conversation. Wait for me in the hall."

It didn't sound like a request. This man was used to giving orders that were obeyed. Embarrassment told me to

INDECISION

flee far and fast, but an impulsive desire to run my hands over his body won out. There was something about him, beyond the insanely hot exterior. Like a spark seeking shelter in the rain, I felt drawn to him. I had no doubt that underneath him, that spark would ignite into a blazing inferno given the chance.

"Okay." My response tumbled out weakly. I hated myself for agreeing so easily, as he'd obviously expected me to. I probably came off like a lovesick puppy starved for attention, happy to get whatever meager scraps I could. The fact was though, I did want to talk to him. Maybe flirt a little. Perhaps steal a kiss or two. Was there really any harm in that? I was a grown woman, single, and yes, maybe a little sexually frustrated. If I wanted to talk to an attractive man, what was there to stop me? For the first time in ten years, I didn't have to consider what example I was setting for my little sister.

I stepped into the darkened hallway. Unable to stand still, I began pacing. A tall, dark-skinned man headed down the hall and went into the men's room. I leaned against the wall and took a deep breath just as Sex on legs exited. I really needed to find out his name before I accidentally verbalized my little nickname to him.

As if reading my mind, he gave me a smile full of charm and character and held out his hand to me. "I'm Max. And you are..." His brow lifted.

My nipples pebbled at the sound of his deep, smooth voice. I took his hand and cleared my throat. "Chloe."

His hand was large and warm. He held on to mine a little longer than necessary, brought it up to his mouth, and placed a soft kiss on my knuckles. A tingling sensation ran up my arm from our point of contact. I looked up into his eyes when he released my hand and gulped. The butterflies in my stomach were working overtime. I'd never really understood what those romance novels I read meant when they said a person could get lost in someone's eyes. But at this moment it all made perfect sense. It was like we were having a conversation without speaking.

"It's a pleasure to meet you, Chloe. Would you be comfortable heading down to one of the VIP rooms to talk? It'd be quieter. Private."

Private. Oh, God. Should I?

He seemed harmless enough, but I was more concerned with myself at the moment. So what if I wanted to claw his clothes right off of him? I wasn't an animal. Surely, I could control myself.

"Um, sure." I shrugged feigning nonchalance. "Just let me go and tell my friends where I am. It's your turn to wait in the hall. I'll be right back."

He laughed, and I pushed off the wall. It took me a moment to fully get my balance. I headed toward the bar area. My limbs felt wooden and my movements stilted under his watchful eye.

When I reached the main room, my pace quickened until I stopped short of the table and motioned Jackie over. She got up, which took some doing. I grabbed her arm to steady her wobbly stance and turned my head to the side when I got a whiff of her vodka-infused breath.

"What's up?" she asked and cocked her head to the side, narrowing her eyes. "Where have you been?"

I pressed a hand to my racing heart. "You're never going to believe who I just met. That guy we were talking about earlier, the one across the room."

Jackie's eyes widened. "That hot piece of eye candy in the suit?"

"Yeah. He's asked me to go with him to one of the private rooms in the back so we can talk, but...I don't know."

She craned her neck back, looking at me like I was

crazy. "Oh, come on. Are you serious? The hottest guy in this place wants to chat you up and you're thinking of turning him down?"

"What if that's not all he wants to do?" I asked with a meaningful look.

"Let's hope it's not. Did you see that guy?" She wagged her eyebrows up and down. I couldn't help the small smile that escaped my lips.

"I don't know anything about him. He could be a serial killer for all I know."

Jackie had a give-me-a-break look plastered on her face.

"We're here for your bachelorette party," I pointed out. "Not for me to pick up some random guy. It's your day."

Not having it, Jackie grabbed both of my shoulders and gave me a small shake. "Have you been tuning me out all night? Nothing would make me happier than seeing you pick up that beautiful piece of man candy tonight. Think of it as an early wedding gift to yours truly." She winked.

I laughed. "You don't mind?"

"Go!" She shooed me away. "Seriously. Have fun for once. You're allowed. Your sister will be leaving for school soon to start her own life, and besides—she isn't here anyway. You don't have to spend every waking moment taking care of everyone else. You didn't have a choice before, but you do now. Have fun. No one here is going to judge you." Her face was serious and her words heartfelt.

Suddenly, I found myself wanting that freedom that Jackie had been trying to shove on me all night. I felt almost...giddy. I hugged my best friend, and Jackie said in my ear, "Keep your phone on you. Don't you dare leave this place with him, and if you're not back in an hour, I'm coming after your ass."

I laughed at her comment and nodded before

heading back to where I'd left Max. His gaze never wavered as I made my way closer to him.

"Everything okay?" he asked.

"I reassured my friends that you didn't seem like the serial killer type, but if I'm not back in an hour they'll send out the search party."

"Let's not waste any time then. I have a feeling an hour won't nearly be long enough."

Need shot through me fast and fierce, concentrating in my core, and images of the two of us in all sorts of sexual positions came to mind. I wasn't even sure they were all anatomically possible. It was all I could do not to fan myself.

He led me down the darkened hallway away from the main room, his hand on my lower back. It was an intimate gesture, and I revelled in the feeling.

With giddy anticipation that I hadn't experienced in a lifetime, it occurred to me that I'd never done anything like this before—go off to a private room with a complete stranger. That sounded more like Jackie than the responsible and driven woman I'd had to be these past ten years. But I *was* in the mood for some fun, flirting, and maybe a make-out session.

What's the worst that could happen?

**Indiscretion is available for purchase at the following retailers:**

Amazon ---> http://bit.ly/1sgvldk
Kobo ---> http://bit.ly/1uvQrKs
B&N ---> http://bit.ly/1ozvyRf
iTunes ---> http://bit.ly/1Epzjbp
Google Play ---> http://bit.ly/1pMDD1a

# INDECISION

www.ingramcontent.com/pod-product-compliance
Lightning Source LLC
Chambersburg PA
CBHW021146130626
46554CB00005B/1693